Who Trespass Against Us

The Untold Story of the Life and Judgment

of the Las Vegas Shooter

&

One Girl's Journey Through

That Dark Night

D. P. Conway

Inspired by Actual Events

To Cindy + Claire,
God bless and I
hope you enjoy!
Don Conway
"D.P."

Day Lights Publishing House, Inc.

Cleveland, Ohio

Copyright & Publication

"Who Trespass Against Us" is a work of fiction based on actual events. All incidents, images, dialogue, and all characters, except for some well-known public figures, are products of the author's imagination and are not to be construed as real. Where real-life historical persons, images, or places appear, the situations, incidents, and dialogues concerning those persons are entirely fictional and are not intended to depict actual events or to change the altogether fictional nature of the work. In all other respects, any resemblance to actual persons, living or deceased, events, institutions, or locales is entirely coincidental.

Day Lights Publishing House, Inc.
5498 Dorothy N. Olmsted OH 44070
www.daylightspublishing.com

Photo sources and credits are listed in the back of the book, and at www.dpconway.com

Cover by Colleen Conway Cooper and Nate Myers

Edited by Connie Swenson

Associate Editors Colleen Conway Cooper and Mary Egan

Story Consultant Edward Markovich

Dedications

For the families, friends, and lovers
of the deceased victims
of the Route 91 Harvest Festival shooting in Las Vegas,
May the Lord hold you close until the forever day
when you will see your loved one again.

For all those who were wounded and
for those who care for them,
May the Lord bless you
and strengthen you
to live on in love.

For Marisa
Io ti amo sempre.

Why I Wrote This Book

On October 1, 2017, Stephen Paddock opened fire. The next day I sat before the TV, stunned, fixated on the news coverage of the mass shooting, desperately trying to understand why he did it.

As I watched, I realized this tragedy narrowly missed our family. In early September my daughter and her friend had flown to Austin, Texas to see her brother, and attend an Eric Church concert. It was only after arriving that they found out the show had been canceled. When she got back home, she tried to find someone to go with her to Las Vegas to see Eric Church perform at the Route 91 Harvest Festival. No one could go, so she decided against it.

She could have been in the crowd in Las Vegas on that dark night. She could have been one of the wounded or even one of those who would never be coming home again.

At the time of the shooting, I was on the verge of publishing the first book of my *After Life* series. I stopped because I realized the years I spent writing the 12 books in the series, had prepared me to write this story.

Five years ago, in April 2012, within days of starting to write the *After Life* series, there was an article in our Cleveland area newspaper about a tragic shooting at a local restaurant. A mother and her young daughter were killed, and one other daughter was severely wounded. As I read, I suddenly realized I knew them, they were my tax clients, who I had seen and spoke to only weeks earlier in my office.

Within a month, the wounded girl died. It was at this time that I was moved to write a fictional story of their life, including imagining the events that led the reclusive husband to commit this horrific crime. But more importantly, I wanted to write the rest of the story, the part about the reuniting of the wounded girl with her mom and sister in Heaven, and their journey into the After Life.

Then six months later, the shooting at Sandy Hook happened, and along with the rest of America, I felt terrible shock and grief. We all felt it. The following day, while watching the news, I became determined to tell the rest of the story, the part we don't hear about, the part that happens after we die. I began with a fictional account of what led Adam Lanza to do his dark deed. I also wrote of the courage of the principal and teachers as they tried to protect the children during the shooting, and of their efforts later to help the children understand their journey into Heaven.

Over the next four years, I wrote 13 more stories. There are a wide variety of people in these stories. There is a mob lawyer, a young girl who has Rett's disease, a woman who was abused as a child, a middle-aged divorced woman, a U.S. Senator, and even an avowed atheist. These and the other stories portray people's lives, struggles, deaths, and crossings over to the afterlife.

Very few have it all together before death suddenly crashes into their plans for life. Many never reach the hopes and dreams they desired and often desperately needed.

The series paints the picture of what happens to them after death, and what possibilities still exist to find those dreams, and how each person fits into the coming war at the end of time. Many of the stories are about second chances and life on the other side, a life we all want.

But some of the stories are cautionary tales, like the mob lawyer's story. Even the 9/11 hijackers are addressed later, in book 10, because the series is not only about Heaven, but also about Hell, and about a place in between, for those who now don't quite fit into Heaven or Hell.

During the same five years, I wrote a much longer story called the Archangel Sagas, which is weaved through, and spans all 12 books of the *After Life* series. It is an epic story of Angels, Archangels, and the Dark Side Angels, whose lives are racing to the final showdown of good and evil.

But then October 1, 2017, came upon us all. Three days after the shooting, my associate called. He said, "I know we're busy trying to get the first book done, and I know we're all in shock at what happened, but I was listening to a radio program last night and could not stop thinking that you should look at this as a possible story. It doesn't exactly fit into the series, but this is the kind of thing we've been writing about for five years now. I think you could make a difference."

I remember sighing when he said it, because, I was already overwhelmed, and already feeling pressured at trying to "launch" my first book. I am a CPA, not a writer. But it was more than that, I was in shock just like everyone else. I said to him, "I appreciate you saying that, but to be honest, I wouldn't even know where to start."

I didn't give it another thought. But the next day after I got up, I decided to look at a few articles. One of the pieces was from the Chicago Tribune. It was about the shooter's father Benny, also known as 'Bingo Bruce.' Reading about the darkness of the father's life helped me to imagine how an evil streak, even if it was kept secret from the recipient, could have been passed down to the shooter.

Over the next week, I did exhaustive research, examining known facts, and filling in the blanks where necessary, to piece together a compelling narrative to provide a possible answer to the question "Why?"

But doing so was only half of my vision. The real reason I wrote this book, was to tell the rest of the story, a story to help see beyond the tragedy. After 3 weeks of writing, I told my wife, "I finished with the Stephen part of the story. Now I am going to see if I can thread the needle and bring hope out of this darkness."

So, I got to work, and used my own daughters' experience of getting into country music as a teen, to help me imagine and present the inspiring story of a young woman and her best friend, both country music fans, who journey together through life and face that dark night together.

There were tears as I wrote the ending. Most of my test readers told me they too, choked up at the end. In hearing this, I knew I had threaded the needle, and I am grateful to God.

I wrote *Who Trespass Against Us* in less than 4 weeks, about the same amount of time that Charles Dickens took to write *A Christmas Carol*. I only knew this because right after finishing, I saw the movie *The Man Who Invented Christmas*. I could not help but feel connected to Dickens, who had a vision for a story, and ran with it 174 years before I did.

Who Trespass Against Us is a work of fiction inspired by real events. It is a gripping account of one of our nation's worst tragedies. But it is also a message of hope, because evil does not win, and death is not the end. It is only the beginning of something... a second chance... a forever chance.

D.P. Conway

December 2017

"Fairy tales do not tell children the dragons exist.

Children already know that dragons exist.

Fairy tales tell children the dragons can be killed."

G.K. Chesterton

Genealogy of the Las Vegas Shooter

"Then Cain killed his brother Abel, and the ground that swallowed Abel's blood cried out to the Lord." -Genesis
"And the Lord put a mark on Cain." -Genesis

Afterward, Cain had relations with his wife, and she conceived and bore the child Enoch.
Enoch begot Irad.
Irad begot Mehujael.
Mehujael begot Mathusael.

Thousands of years later…

William Bury had relations with his wife, and she conceived and bore the child Mason, who was later adopted.
Mason Paddock begot Benjamin.
Benjamin Paddock begot Stephen.
Stephen Paddock begot no one.

Stephen's seed is stricken from the earth.

OPENING STATEMENT

I am Thaddus.

Six thousand years ago I was an Angel in the Heavens until I foolishly took part in the Great Rebellion. Now, I am a Dark Angel, and at the time of this writing, there is little hope I will ever be anything else.

There is something I need to confess to you about the events in Las Vegas on October 1, 2017. I was Stephen Paddock's Dark Angel, and I admit that on that night, I was there.

People don't realize it, but we are always there.

I was assigned to his family line centuries ago, and I tell you truly, this event had its roots long before Stephen Paddock did his dark deed. I am picking up the story in Dundee, Scotland because that's where things got going. It is, as they say, the "beginning of the matter."

The most important thing I want you to understand is that I did the unthinkable for a Dark Angel. I tried to stop him, and I will say this at my trial.

The real story of everything that happened is set down in these pages. Why do I say this? Because I am the only one who knows the whole story. I am the only one who was there from the start. Whether or not you believe me, that is up to you.

CHAPTER 1

1889 Dundee Scotland

"No, Mrs. Marjory, we have no other children, just wee little Mason here," Ellen Bury said in her thick Scottish accent.

"Aye, he's a handsome little boy, how old is he?" asked Mrs. Marjory.

"He's only one month and smart as a whip, mind you," Ellen said, as she sat in the little shop on Prince Street cradling the infant in her arms.

Mrs. Marjory sipped her tea and glanced out the window at the cold rainy January day. "And ye traveled all the way from Whitechapel London with him only being' one month old, did ye?"

"Ahhh, yes. We had to leave straight away, there was no time to tarry." Ellen looked up and saw her husband William in the distance. "Oh, here comes my husband now."

Mrs. Marjory turned toward the window, pausing momentarily. Something about the man rattled her, though she didn't know what. Maybe it was his eyes; they were cold and dark. They held something, an emptiness perhaps, but one filled with hatred and evil. But then the man smiled at her, and the feeling went away as quickly as it had come.

William Bury walked into the shop, located underneath the upstairs flat for rent. Ellen stood up to introduce her husband, "William, this is the landlady, Mrs. Marjory. She says the place is still available and will cost five shillings a month."

William put on his fake smile and nodded. "Pleased to meet you, Mrs. Marjory. We will take it."

Mrs. Marjory's eyes widened a bit, "Aye, you'll take it will ye." She paused, and clasped her hands together, thinking, then said, "From Whitechapel, you say, hmmm." She paused again, trying to form the right words for her question. She then asked, "Well what sort of work was this you Whitechapel people have been about… letting Jack the Ripper kill so many?"

William Bury kept his smile fixed, but inwardly he wanted to grab her by the throat. The rage rose faster than ever. Ellen saw him reacting. She felt the tension and placed her hand on his arm, laughing, "Well from all I've heard, Mrs. Marjory, Jack the Ripper is quiet now, and I have a feeling it'll stay that way."

"Oh, ye do, do ye," Mrs. Marjory said, rolling her eyes. "Well… we'll see I suppose."

There was silence as the three stood inside the front of Mrs. Marjory's store and flat. Ellen broke the silence, "Well may we have the place?"

Mrs. Marjory paused for a moment, then nodded. "Aye, why sure ye can, here is the key. I'll open a little account for ye at my store so you can get started."

"That won't be necessary," said William as he briskly turned toward the door, leaving Mrs. Marjory to hand the keys to Ellen.

Three weeks later

Ellen glanced over at the fireplace where William was sitting, sipping a bottle of whiskey, whittling a piece of wood with his knife. She sat silently at the kitchen table, knitting booties for her baby, as little Mason lay asleep in a small bassinette next to her.

Suddenly William stood up and abruptly announced, "I'm goin' out for a while."

Ellen's eyes widened, she heard the tension in his voice. She put her knitting down and immediately stood up to face him. "No, no you said that was it. No more going out William."

The tension began to turn to rage, the voice of rage William had known since he was a child, the voice that tormented him until he found the way to calm it. He walked over to her, "What do you mean 'No'? I *am* going out."

Ellen pleaded, "You promised me, William. I… I will tell them."

"You will what?" he gritted his teeth as his voice suddenly changed, "You will what now?"

Ellen backed up, grabbed the baby, and ran into the bedroom.

William set down the bottle of whiskey loudly on the table, gripped the knife, picked up a small piece of rope from beside the fireplace, and slowly walked toward the door.

He paused, his conscience telling him 'no,' yet he felt his rage boiling and his eyes glowing red with heat. Destiny was screaming in his mind. He opened the door. Ellen was cowering, sitting on the bed, watching him as he stepped closer. She looked at the knife and the rope, and quickly put the baby into the bassinette. "William, please. You… you… don't have to…" He grabbed her, and she began to plead with him, "No William… please."

The following morning William sat quietly at the kitchen table, periodically looking through the slightly ajar door into the bedroom. He glanced down at little Mason asleep in the bassinette next to him. Suddenly William stood, tormented, and began to pace the floor. Ellen was the only woman who ever truly loved him, he knew this now.

He heard the door of the downstairs shop unlock and open. He looked at the clock, it was Mrs. Marjory opening the store.

Mrs. Marjory walked across the floor to the back of the shop, and suddenly slid, nearly falling. She caught herself and looked down. There was a puddle of something on the floor. She held the lamp looking closer. Her eyes widened, just as a drop of blood fell onto her white sleeve. She looked up at the ceiling, and gasped, then ran out and to find the police.

Five minutes later a policeman blowing a whistle, came running up the stairs. He kicked open the door and saw William sitting at the table with a blank look on his face. The policeman looked in the bedroom and immediately ordered William to lay flat on the floor. Within minutes more police arrived. They cuffed William and hauled him to the Dundee Prison. They then began the grim task of carrying Ellen's bloody body away.

Mason was quietly taken away too. The judge ordered that nothing of the child should be in the news, and the newspaper editor honored that request. Mrs. Marjory asked for temporary custody of little Mason and was granted it. Within several weeks the next of kin in England were contacted.

CHAPTER 2

April 24, 1889, Dundee Prison

A crowd of nearly 300 people from as far away as London, walked behind the condemned man. Some were crying, some trying to get his attention, but most were jeering, excited that Bury would now get justice. Even though William Bury had only confessed to killing Ellen, many had traveled from Whitechapel, believing he was guilty of much more.

The Dark Angel Thaddus stood on top of the prison building looking down upon the gallows. His black wings glistened in the steady rain of the cold, cloudy day. William was his responsibility, and so far, all was going according to plan.

Just then, an Angel named David from the other side landed next to him. "Ash, hello Thaddus. Will today be the day you join the other Dark Angels who are imprisoned in the cages?"

Thaddus smugly glanced over at him, "I doubt it."

"Well, I don't. I'm going to get William to confess to it all and get him to ask the Lords for forgiveness. Once he does, it won't go well for you. You WILL face the wrath of the Lords."

Thaddus half smiled, shaking his head, "I've told you, you're wrong. They are only rumors because he lived there."

David smiled, "We will see, won't we?" David leaped into the air and flew down for his final chance to sway William Bury.

Thaddus watched him, and for a moment lamented he'd been assigned to this man. He had no control over the voice of the Dark Lord that drove men, especially men who bore the dark mark, to commit the most heinous of crimes.

Deep down though, Thaddus wasn't too worried. He was two steps ahead of them all. Since he was hanging anyway, William wanted to confess to all the killings, but Thaddus had convinced him not to, by promising William only a short stay in Hell. It was a lie of course, but that was what Dark Angels did, they lied. Still, there was a chance his plan could backfire, there was still time for it all to unravel.

Thaddus nervously flew closer, hovering over the crowd, watching his dejected client lumber along the final stretch of the muddy walkway. Thaddus breathed a sigh of relief as William reached the gallows, paused to stare up, then resolutely climbed the 12 wide wooden stairs to the hanging platform. His time was running out.

The Angel David was hovering over William, pleading into his mind for him to confess and ask forgiveness, but William's angry face showed he would not.

When William reached the top step, he turned to face the four men who stood waiting on the platform. These were men with official duties to make sure all was done in accordance with proper hanging procedure. Two of them held William, while the other two fixed the noose around William's neck. They tightened it and asked if he had any final words.

William stood silently as all eyes were now fixed on him. He heard his conscience pleading with him to ask forgiveness. He was thinking it over, as he looked out over the crowd, confused, but then his eyes locked on Thaddus, Thaddus was nodding, urging him on. William trusted Thaddus, and he trusted the deal they had struck.

He decided to make a show for the crowd and began to grin as if some unexpected joyful news had just arrived. He let out a sinister laugh, and shouted, "No more the sun! Into the dark, I go!"

A deafening silence swept over the crowd, followed by murmuring. Many felt something demonic had just been uttered. The hangman did not wonder or ponder his meaning. He forcefully pulled the lever, surprising all in the tense moment. William's body dropped down, stopping with a horrendous thud. After several minutes of shuddering and twirling, all grew still.

Thaddus waited a moment, basking in the sense of satisfaction he felt. He had successfully guided a man with the dark mark into Hell, without him being found guilty of all the heinous crimes some wished to label him with.

Thaddus smiled, then swooped down and drove a large hook into the back of William, lifting the dead man into the sky. "Wake up William. It's time to go to Hell."

William woke in agony and began to scream, "Stop! It hurts!"

"Oh, I know it hurts William." Thaddus laughed.

William's eyes widened, "Wait, you said… it will only be for a short time, right?"

"Yes William, a short time it will be… till we get there, then… it might seem like forever." Thaddus started laughing, as a look of horror came over William's face.

One Month Later

A horse-drawn carriage pulled up to the courthouse. Mr. and

Mrs. James Paddock, cousins of Ellen from England, climbed out and went inside. They were there to take custody of Mason. Mrs. Marjory, who had been taking care of the child, was there waiting in an adjoining room with the bundled baby. She took the bottle of holy water from her pocket and put a drop on the baby's forehead one more time, tracing the sign of the cross and uttering the ancient prayer an old woman from the village had given her. Mrs. Marjory had performed this ritual every day since the killing. She put the holy water back in her pocket and closed her eyes, knowing it would be the last time.

After the Paddock's signed the papers, a door was opened, and Mrs. Marjory brought the child in. She quietly handed the sleeping baby to Mrs. Paddock. Mrs. Marjory then went back into the adjoining room and dragged in a small trunk of things that belonged to Ellen. She also handed them a large envelope.

"What is this?" asked Mr. Paddock.

"Aye, it's newspaper clippings from the trial... and some other things I found that I thought would be of interest to ye."

Mr. Paddock thanked her. But Mrs. Marjory did not smile. It was as if she needed to tell him something more, something important. "Mr. and Mrs. Paddock, I... I wanted... "She stopped, knowing she might be labeled as a loon. "Never mind," she said.

The Paddock family took Mason back to England where they were preparing to emigrate to America. Mason would be going with them.

CHAPTER 3

1921 Sheboygan Wisconsin... 33 Years Later

Mason Paddock looked through the hospital ward window at the cribs. There were seven babies, but he was deep in contemplation with his eyes fixed on the fourth child. A little sign taped to the crib read, "Baby Boy Paddock."

Mason felt the pride of new life, he was 33 years old, and his wife had just given them their first child. But he was worried. He hadn't had time for anything between working and getting to the hospital each night. It was their third day there, and his wife and child would be coming home. He needed to get home. He needed to see the letter again.

After signing the hospital discharge papers and loading his wife and child into his car, he drove toward home. As the sun set on the distant horizon, he could not help but feel hope for the future. His wife and newborn son Benjamin were coming home today.

Mason had fought bravely in WWI and had earned numerous medals of distinction. A lieutenant in the Army, he regretted having sent two hundred men to their deaths. They were serving the cause of freedom, the cause of America. Mason trusted that they all knew this when they raced up ladders out of the trenches. Because of their sacrifice, America had come out the victor, and he was now home, enjoying the fruits of freedom. He vowed never to forget them.

He pulled onto the gravel drive of their little bungalow that backed up to the Pigeon River. He helped his young wife and child upstairs and into bed. He and his wife talked a while, reading together in bed.

After she fell asleep, he got out of bed and went down into his workshop. He turned on the light and pulled out a small wooden box he had kept hidden from his wife. It was his mother's. It was something she had always kept hidden. As a boy, he knew she kept it locked, so he never saw what was inside until after she died.

He rifled through the clippings. He had seen them plenty of times over the past year. He paused to look again at the picture he now believed was his real father being led to the gallows. There was nothing more to see, he had studied it many times, looking for clues. But tonight, he was looking for the letter. He had read it countless times but now needed to reread it. He carefully unfolded the parched worn-out paper.

June 3rd, 1889

Dundee Scotland

Dear Mr. and Mrs. Paddock,

I've been wrestling with the idea as to whether I should tell ye my opinion of what happened here last winter.

Ellen was a beautiful woman, and so was her baby. But ye see, it was the husband who was more than just a killer. He was evil I tell ye. The local funeral man told me that William Bury indeed had the mark on his body, sure as day. I could never know this myself, but I do know of the darkness I saw in his eyes, and in his soul.

He came from Whitechapel, and from the day he arrived, the infamous killings by Jack the Ripper in Whitechapel stopped. I believe he was Jack the Ripper. I am almost certain of it. There's no proof, except I understand now, what Ellen meant when she told me that she believed "Jack the Ripper would be quiet now."

She didn't say it directly, but it was because she had gotten him out of Whitechapel. I believe with all my heart that poor Ellen knew who her husband was, and THAT is WHY he killed her.

I took care of the baby for a month or so, and I bathed the little fella lots of times. I am sure he did NOT have the mark. But I talked to a local woman, steeped in the knowledge of the dark side. She told me in no uncertain terms that the Mark of Cain can never be wiped off the earth, and she told me that dark lore held his race would always live on.

And it is because of this, I plead with ye, to watch all children that may come from this little boy. Watch them I tell ye, and if they have the mark, beware. I hesitate to say, but it may be better if they never were born at all.

As God is my witness,

Mrs. Marjory

Mason stared at the letter for a long while, thinking. He folded it and placed it inside the box. He pulled out the other letter, the one he kept behind it. It was not nearly as worn, nor as old, but it was just as important. He unfolded it and began to read.

March 27th, 1908

Sheboygan Wisconsin

My Dear Mason,

I know someday you will find this box with all these clippings and letters related to your real father. I decided I best write this, in case something happens to me.

Why did I keep the letter from Mrs. Marjory all these years? It's because I want you to understand things for yourself my boy and make up your own mind. You have the right to know your bloodline. Things like this are never buried for good. I wanted you to hear it from your mother.

Mrs. Marjory was a crazy woman and is not to be believed. From the moment I met her, I knew there was something off about her. Indeed, after reading her letter, I had correspondence with the Chief Constable in Dundee. His replies are included in this box. He too thought her mad.

They say she committed suicide by throwing herself off a cliff into the sea. There were no witnesses, only that she told her friends she loved that place and would go there often. She was seen walking down the road alone towards the cliff the day she went missing for good.

The constable told me that from the time your real mother, Ellen, was killed, Mrs. Marjory was near daily at his door with her wild claims. Yes, it's true she was not the only one who believed it, but I think others merely grabbed onto her fantasies. I tried to find out who the local woman was she referred to as steeped in matters of the dark side, but never could find her.

I'll tell you now, this whole Mark of Cain nonsense isn't true. I've watched you since you were a baby and there is no mark of any kind upon you. Only the mark of a mother and father's love. It doesn't matter who your real parents were, it was your father and me who raised you and made you who you are today.

With all my love,

Mom

Mason took a deep breath and sighed. He had doubts, but he needed to check Benjamin. Mason closed his eyes for a moment, then folded his mother's letter and went upstairs. He walked to the bassinette where his sleeping son lay. He stared for a while, looking, wondering, then picked him up. The boy woke up fussing.

"Is he OK?" the baby's mother asked.

"Yes, go back to sleep. His diaper just needs changing, I'll do it."

His wife nodded, and gratefully fell back asleep. He took the boy downstairs and turned on the light in the living room. He laid him on a blanket on the floor and fetched a new diaper. He undressed him, and carefully examined the front of his body. He turned the boy over, then froze. He got up and set the lamp on the floor.

There on the back of the boy, just near the top of the hip, was a small cloud shaped mark. It was faint, but it was there. Mrs. Marjory's words flashed through his mind. *It might be better if he were never born.* He objected to himself out loud. "No, no… no, I won't."

He looked again, confirming what he saw, then turned the boy over and smiled, "Don't you worry Benjamin. I'll be keeping you in line. There'll be no straying from the straight and narrow road for you. If it's the last thing I do, I'll make sure you become a model citizen."

1 *William and Ellen Bury Home, Dundee, Scotland*

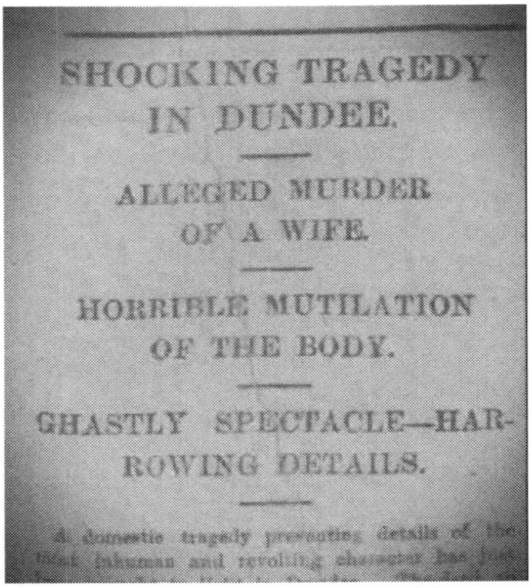

SHOCKING TRAGEDY IN DUNDEE.

ALLEGED MURDER OF A WIFE.

HORRIBLE MUTILATION OF THE BODY.

GHASTLY SPECTACLE—HARROWING DETAILS.

A domestic tragedy presenting details of the most inhuman and revolting character has just

2 *News clipping of Ellen's murder*

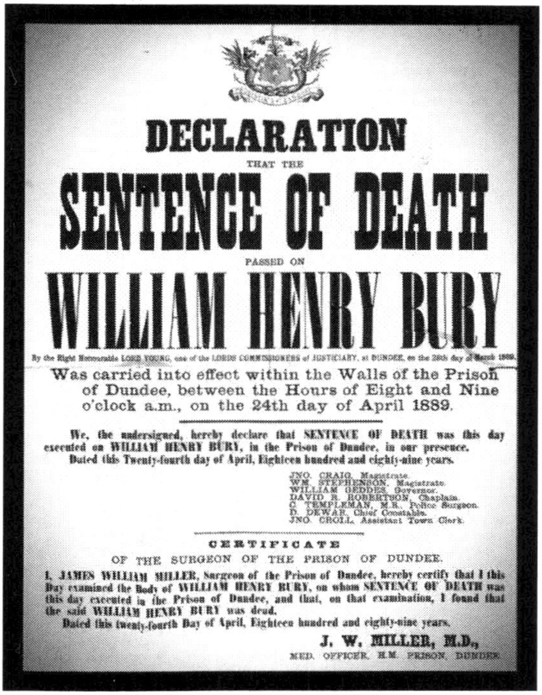

DECLARATION
THAT THE
SENTENCE OF DEATH
PASSED ON
WILLIAM HENRY BURY

By the Right Honourable LORD YOUNG, one of the LORDS COMMISSIONERS of JUSTICIARY, at DUNDEE, on the 28th day of March 1889.

Was carried into effect within the Walls of the Prison of Dundee, between the Hours of Eight and Nine o'clock a.m., on the 24th day of April 1889.

We, the undersigned, hereby declare that SENTENCE OF DEATH was this day executed on WILLIAM HENRY BURY, in the Prison of Dundee, in our presence.
Dated this Twenty-fourth day of April, Eighteen hundred and eighty-nine years.

JNO. CRAIG, Magistrate.
WM. STEPHENSON, Magistrate.
WILLIAM GEDDES, Governor.
DAVID R. ROBERTSON, Chaplain.
C. TEMPLEMAN, M.B., Police Surgeon.
D. DEWAR, Chief Constable.
JNO. CROLL, Assistant Town Clerk.

CERTIFICATE
OF THE SURGEON OF THE PRISON OF DUNDEE.

I, JAMES WILLIAM MILLER, Surgeon of the Prison of Dundee, hereby certify that I this Day examined the Body of WILLIAM HENRY BURY, on whom SENTENCE OF DEATH was this day executed in the Prison of Dundee, and that, on that examination, I found that the said WILLIAM HENRY BURY was dead.
Dated this twenty-fourth Day of April, Eighteen hundred and eighty-nine years.

J. W. MILLER, M.D.,
MED. OFFICER, H.M. PRISON, DUNDEE.

3 Sentence of Death for William Bury

4 Dundee Hanging Platform, 12 steps, 4 men wait, condemned man's arm held by a priest wearing a white robe.

5 *Mrs. Marjory of Dundee, shortly before she went missing*

CHAPTER 4

1979 Springfield Oregon . . . 58 Years Later

"Bingo, what do ya say we move on down the road soon? They're gonna catch on before long, don't you think?" asked Mary in her Chicago accent, as she sat drinking coffee at the kitchen table.

Bingo grinned that sinister grin he'd worn since he was a teenager. "Yeah, I suppose you're right Mary. We'll milk it a little longer here. In the spring, we'll pull up stakes, maybe go set up somewhere down in good old Texas."

"Ease on down the road to Texas with all our dough. Ha!" A broad, confident smile came across her face. Mary Jaycox was just shy of 57 and sexy as ever. She was slim, good-looking, and kept her hair colored the same dark black she'd had since they met. The rest was Mother Nature being kind to her.

Bingo walked over, picked her up, and lifted her onto the dryer located off the kitchen in their double-wide trailer. "Mary Jaycox, you do know how to inspire me." Bingo Bruce just turned 58, but at 6'4" and 250 lbs. he had no trouble lifting Mary, especially when he had on hard-on for her. He unbuttoned her white nylon pants and helped her slip them off. Mary put her arms around his neck, and lifted herself up, making it easier for him. "I'm here for you Bingo," she said, staring into his big blue eyes. "I'm always yours for the takin'."

Bingo Bruce, as he was called by the locals, was a con man, although they didn't know. He had been way more than that, but they didn't know that either. Old age was mellowing him, but to his core, he was a criminal. He'd been a bank robber, a murderer, and a mob thug for most of his life.

He pushed himself firmly into Mary once more, feeling her clutching him tightly as her body quaked. "That's it, Mary, stay right… there." Finally, his body released, and he backed away and lifted her down. "You still got it, Mary, you still make me crazy."

It was time to get ready for his weekly bingo game where he was known and loved by all. His real name was Benjamin Paddock.

The notion of becoming a criminal first settled on Benny 40 years earlier. It was a cold morning outside their basement apartment in Chicago. Benny was only 15 and had stolen some jewelry from a local store. It was easy, he just reached his hand over the counter, grabbed some necklaces, and ran. The beat cop saw him running, and whacked him with his club, stopping him cold. Because of Benny's age, the owner would not press charges, but the cop brought Benny home to his father, Mason Paddock.

Mason apologized for his son, thanked the cop, and waited for him to leave. As soon as he did, Mason promptly took Benny outside and beat the hell out of him. Benny would never forget the feeling of cold snow pressing on his bruised cheek. He thought he was going to die but learned a valuable lesson that day. He'd get back at his father for beating him by becoming what his father loathed. He could get back at his father by being a criminal, and in that cold snow, he vowed to do it.

Benny met Mary 13 years later in the Green Mill Cocktail Lounge in Chicago. It was 1949, and he was 28 years old. He had already become a reliable low-level man in the Chicago mob. World War II was only a few years over, and life and crime were back in full swing. Mary was a cocktail waitress working to make money and meet men, but mainly to meet men. She knew money would follow the right man. Mary was petite, with dark black curly hair. Most nights she wore a tight white half-buttoned blouse, fishnet stockings, and a short green puffed skirt that plopped up nicely in the back when she bent over. Her outfit magnified all her assets.

The first night Benny met her, he tipped her $20, which was a lot of money in those days. He asked her to come out with him after her shift, and she said yes. Before the night was over, he laid her in his car. To Benny, it was more than a one-night stand. He fell in love with her that night. While it took a good number of months longer for her to reciprocate, she eventually fell in love with him.

Mary had other lovers, but there was something about Benny she found irresistible. Perhaps it was the easy lies he told her. She didn't know for sure which ones really were lies, and which ones were true. But it didn't matter to her, because he was good at it, and he kept things exciting, and he was also a fantastic lover. But she wouldn't marry him, she had others on the side, nothing serious, but they kept her in money and kept her regularly laid.

But as the year passed, it was Benny that Mary grew to love the most. After a year she ended the other relationships, and Benny began keeping an apartment for her. He gave her all the money, sex and excitement she needed, she had only to be his girl.

Benny confided sparingly with her about all his dealings, and Mary found herself increasingly intrigued by her 'bad boy' boyfriend.

CHAPTER 5

One night Benny revealed something in his soul to Mary, something that scared her, and yet at the same time, turned her on.

They were in Halligans on North Lincoln Avenue. Benny had gone up to the bar to get their drinks while Mary sat at a table near the back, looking around at all the finely dressed men and women. It was mainly a mob hangout, but not exclusively. Many of the men cast a glance or two her way, and she didn't mind, it made her feel pretty. She glanced over at Benny wondering what was taking him so long and saw he was talking to a couple of sailors at the bar. They were in uniform, not too young, maybe in their 30's. Mary figured they were probably veterans of the war.

Suddenly, there was a scuffle. Mary watched as Benny threw a punch, narrowly missing the ducking sailor. The sailor struck back, hitting Benny in the eye. Benny went for his gun, but a bunch of mob goons stopped him.

"Get off me!" Benny shouted as they dragged him outside.

Mary watched as the manager came up and told the sailors to leave, out the back. She waited a moment, then went outside. Benny was arguing with some of the goons. She could tell he knew them. One of them said, "Go home Benny, just forget those guys."

They turned and saw Mary, and said, "Take him home... now!"

Mary nodded, as Benny shrugged them off. She took him by the arm, and they walked to his car and got in. Mary turned on the light and said, "Let me see that eye."

"Bastards!" shouted Benny, slamming his open hands against the dashboard.

"I said let me see that eye Benny!"

He clenched his teeth, looking over at her. He closed his eyes and let her have a look. Mary took a handkerchief out of her purse, spit on it, and began dabbing the blood away. He was cut, but he was more than that, she had never seen him this angry.

"What happened in their Benny?"

"Goddamn sailors, they think they're God's gift."

"What'd you say to them, Benny?"

"I told 'em I thought the war was a waste of good American lives."

"Benny, you can't... "

He pulled away, "I can do whatever the hell I want."

Mary turned and sat deeper in her seat, pissed off that he scolded her. An uneasy silence followed.

Benny grimaced, "We're all Americans, not just the ones who wear it on their damn sleeve."

"I don't know why you're so mad. Those sailors did nothing wrong."

Benny didn't reply.

Mary then said, "I know you got goodness in you, Benny, I know." Mary did see small glimmers of goodness in him, at least in the way he pampered her. She also suspected there was another side, she just didn't want to know about it.

"I'm not as good as you think Mary. I've done some things… some bad things."

"Like what?" she asked, thinking he had only been around the edges of the crime syndicates.

"Remember the Shedrake job at the Buick plant in '42. It was in all the papers. I was in on it, there were five of us, and we took over $14,000. The government said it was $20,000. I think those FBI rats took the other $6,000. I was told to kill one of the guards, but I decided differently, and only wounded him. Mr. Touhy was pissed off, he wanted someone killed, he wanted to make a name for himself with the mob. But I made a joke to make everyone laugh, and the money we got smoothed things over. I was scared for a while, with those FBI rats looking for us. I was afraid someone was gonna turn, but we knew what would happen if we did. Better we trust Mr. Touhy than the damn government."

"Who is Mr. Touhy?"

"He's a mid-level boss, I ran in his crew for a few years." He paused, thinking, then asked," Do you remember when the cops gunned down Ralphy Weinberg?"

"Yes, I do." Mary said, raising her eyes, "I remember the pictures. But he… he was older, wasn't he?"

"Yeah, he was, but he was someone I knew. When I was a young boy, maybe eight or nine, I looked up to Ralphy. He lived in the flat near us. He was kind of like my hero. Ralphy used to give me money and candy, and he always had a pretty girl with him. He tried to rob that Golden Rod Ice Cream Company. I still go by there and cringe when I picture him laying' there, all shot up by those cops, I'll never forget it. Word was, someone tipped them cops off."

"Really, do you know who?" Mary could not believe that Benny was connected to the backstory of such a famous event.

"It was our neighbor, Mr. Miller. He was an army vet, a patriotic yahoo from the First War like my father. He was always watching' for people stepping out of patriotic line. He used to come to our house and talk with dad about the war. I know Mr. Miller hated me. I stared him down after Ralphy was killed, I told him a thing or two." Benny was lying. Yes, he hated Mr. Miller, but he never said a word to him, although in his mind he pinned the tip-off to the cops on him.

Mary was surprised to hear all of this. But she sensed Benny was boasting. "Is that all, cause that's not too bad?"

"No... that's not all," Benny said, disappointed he had not impressed her enough yet. He needed to impress her. He felt low tonight; he needed to feel important. He went on without further hesitation. "I did a job for Paul Ricca not too long ago."

"The Waiter?" exclaimed Mary. Everyone knew who Paul Ricca was.

"Yes, that's right, Paul Ricca, 'The Waiter'... crime boss. We did that bank job on West Madison Street."

Mary exclaimed with alarm in her voice, "Benny... someone was killed there."

"Yeah, I know. I was the one who killed him. I had to. He was some security guard, trying to be a hero. I feel bad sometimes, but it was him or me. I guess I was lucky. I found out in the papers he was an ex-army man. Where the hell do these war vets come off, all trying to be heroes?"

There was quiet for a while. This was news to Mary that Benny had killed someone. Still, she was in too deep to let that bother

her, and besides, she knew he might not even be telling her the truth. She asked, "*Why* are you telling me all this Benny?"

"Because I want you to know about me… why I do the things I do."

"Well, why do you, Benny?" Mary asked softly, running her finger along his thigh. Benny stared out the window, "because, I'm better than him."

"Better than *who*?"

"Better than my old man, that's who. He thinks he's better than me. 'Patriotic government-loving show-off,' that's what I call him. I'd tell him to his face if he didn't die." The truth was Benny was afraid of his old man, and too scared to ever confront him.

He turned toward Mary, "He wanted me to save his honor and join the army when I was only 20. Join the goddamn army so he could look like a Patriot, can you believe that bullshit? I figured, why should I go off to war to defend America." Benny would not tell her that he had been drafted but was found to be mentally unfit. It was another reason he hated both his father and the military.

Benny continued, "My friends joined up, they got their damn heads blown off. They wrote to me, they told me the war was bullshit. They had a commander who ordered them around, ordered them to go up front, ordered them to take the brunt of it. They knew it was going to cost them, they told me in their letters, and it did. But the army said they had to follow orders or get shot! Hell no, not for me! I hate the government, I hate the FBI, I hate the cops, and I hate all the self-righteous patriots who think they're better than me."

Before Mary could say anything, Benny continued. "You want to know something' funny? During the war, my old man worked in the Quarter Master Corp downtown. He brought me down there a few times, he was trying to get me motivated. One time I stole a pack of official Quarter Master stationary. Do you know I used that stationery to rip off the government? I stole 22 cars in 23 months, right off the street, and got paid from the government for every single one of them using that stationary. I wrote to the army, sent in the title papers they had in their glove compartments and said that I, a quartermaster, officially 'purchased them for the war effort!'"

He turned to her with his eyes lit up, and a wide smile on his face. "They never knew the whole story."

"Who?" asked Mary, suddenly not following.

"The cops, the government, they're all the same. Yeah, they busted me, and I confessed to stealing 12 of the cars, only because I personally cashed those checks. The confession got me out of a long jail sentence. But what the government didn't know was they sent me 22 checks. I had 10 of them put into a fake name, and I cashed them separately. Benny shook his head, smiling, "I loved getting' away with that one."

"But wait… you said you got caught."

"Yeah, I got caught for the 12 cars, but I got away with the other 10. I spent a year in Joliet, but it was a good year. No one fucked with me. We had lots of guys loyal to Paul Ricca inside. One time, I had a broad in there. Yeah, we had the guards paid off, and they snuck her in just for me. I'll never forget that night. I was aching'!" Benny was lying, no one was brought in for him.

"Stop it." Mary hit him on the arm in a gesture of playfulness.

"What?" Benny smirked, then paused, as if suddenly lost in thought, gazing out the front windshield at the Chicago night skyline. "You know, my old man didn't care. He never came to see me, and he wrote me twice, telling me what a disgrace I was to the American flag. Screw him! I think he tipped them off to me. I can't prove it, but if he were alive, I'd beat it outta him."

Mary had heard enough, so she gently said, "I'm sorry all this happened Benny, but let's go home now. I'm aching for you, and I can't wait any longer."

Benny nodded and started the car. He drove to her apartment, and they went up. Mary walked in, threw her coat and purse aside, and said, "You get ready, I'm going to take a quick bath and be right out."

Benny grabbed her and kissed her. "Don't take long now."

"I won't."

Benny lit a cigarette, and sat in the chair, listening to the bath water running. He finished his cigarette and undressed and stretched out on the bed. Five minutes later, the bathroom door opened, and Mary stepped out wearing a thigh-high pink robe. She walked to the foot of the bed and stood before him. Benny immediately started getting excited as he watched her gazing at him. Mary slowly unfolded her robe, watching Benny's eyes explore her body. She loved showing off for him. She slowly crept onto the bed like a cat and worked her way up kissing him. "I'm driving tonight Benny. You just lay back and get ready for the ride of your life."

6 *Mary Jaycox age 29*

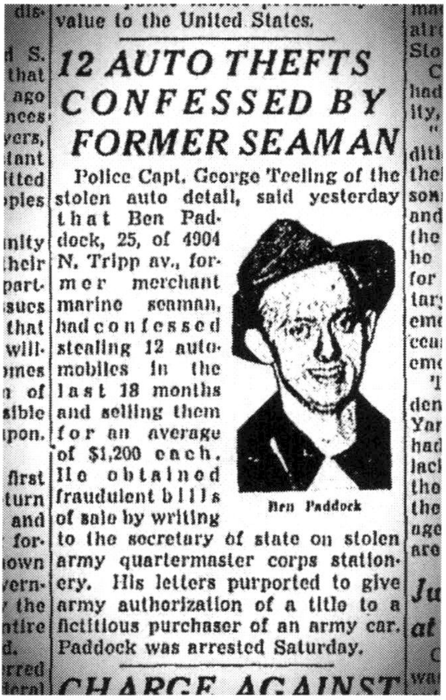

value to the United States.

12 AUTO THEFTS CONFESSED BY FORMER SEAMAN

Police Capt. George Teeling of the stolen auto detail, said yesterday that Ben Paddock, 25, of 4904 N. Tripp av., former merchant marine seaman, had confessed stealing 12 automobiles in the last 18 months and selling them for an average of $1,200 each. He obtained fraudulent bills of sale by writing to the secretary of state on stolen army quartermaster corps stationery. His letters purported to give army authorization of a title to a fictitious purchaser of an army car. Paddock was arrested Saturday.

Ben Paddock

CHARGE AGAINST

7 *Benny Age 25*

8 *Ralphy Weinberg outside the Golden Rod Ice Cream Co.*

9 *Paul "the Waiter" Ricca*

10 *Roger Touhy and Gang*

CHAPTER 6

The following day Benny woke up and saw that Mary had already dressed and left for work. The conversation the night before had brought back to mind things he had not thought of in a long time. It was the voice, the mysterious voice in his head he had heard a few times in his life. He lit a cigarette and let his memory float back to the first time he listened to the voice.

He was only a boy, maybe ten years old and living in Sheboygan on the street called Flower Drive, near the end of Mill Street. Their house and yard backed up to the Pigeon River. There was a stray cat that would lurk around the yard. Benny would bring it milk and occasionally pet it when it wasn't skittish.

He remembered clearly the day it happened. It was a brisk fall morning when a voice began to whisper in his mind. It was soothing and dark. Benny liked it, and he wondered about it. But only hours later he felt a rage, a swelling anger he could not abate. It went on for days until somehow, the voice came back and whispered how to stop it.

The next morning, Benny coaxed the stray cat with milk and snatched it. He ran back by the river, pulled out his large pocket knife, and plunged the blade into the cat's throat, slicing as deep as he could. He dropped the cat and stepped back, watching it die. It made him feel better; it stopped the rage.

Benny left the cat by the river, cleaned the knife, and put it away. The next day he went down to see the cat's carcass. As he was looking at it, the voice came back, friendly and soothing at first, but it quickly brought back the feeling of rage. Benny went into the shed and got the long steel skewers they used for barbecuing. He rammed one down the dead cat's throat and propped it upright into the ground, pounding the rod deep into the dirt. He tied its bloodied outstretched paws to another skewer perpendicular to the first and tied them together.

Benny stepped back, marveling at his homemade crucifix. The rage went away; he felt better again. As he stood admiring what he had done, he heard another voice. "What the hell are you doing?"

Benny turned in shock, it was his father, Mason. Mason walked up, looked at the cat, and looked at his son with a horrified expression. Mason gritted his teeth and grabbed Benny by the hair, angrily beating the living hell out of him. Benny wailed, but he knew how fulfilled he felt at having crucified the cat. Listening to the voice had been worth it.

They took him to the doctor, and he had to explain. But he wouldn't tell the truth, the voice told him not to. Instead, he made an excuse saying one of his friends told him about crucifying cats. He wouldn't say which friend, and when he got home, Mason beat the hell out of him again. Benny knew right then that he could never be broken, and it made him feel strong.

Benny shook out of his daydream and took a long drag from what was left of his cigarette. He crushed it in the ashtray and glanced out the window, thinking about getting going on his day. But then he remembered the other time in his life he had heard the voice. He lit another cigarette and leaned back against the headboard. He closed his eyes, trying to remember, thinking back to the night.

He was 25 years old and in a bar in downtown Chicago. Mark Jeffries, a low-level member of a rival mob family, was down at the other end of the bar drinking and bragging. Benny watched Jeffries for a long time, then he heard the voice for the first time in ages, whispering in his mind that Mark had to die. Benny knew it was the same voice from long ago, and he knew it was a test, a re-awakening that he could brush aside if he wanted. But he didn't, he didn't want to.

Benny waited till Mark left the bar, then followed at a distance. When Mark neared St. Boniface Cemetery, Benny walked up from behind and put his gun in Mark's ribs. "Come with me, and you won't get hurt." Benny forced him into the cemetery, and they walked through the grass, to the middle of the graves.

Benny pressed the gun hard into Mark's back and said, "Now stop and keep looking straight ahead. I just have to ask you one question, then you can go."

Mark nodded, "go ahead, ask."

Benny leaned down, and with his other hand, pulled his long-blade knife out of his sock, and rammed it into Jeffries' neck, pushing it all the way through. He quickly put the side of his gun against the other side of Jeffries' head, squeezing it in a vice-like grip, preventing him from pulling away. Benny held the quivering man firmly, then twisted the blade, listening to the Mark choke on his own blood, feeling him fade, waiting for him to die. Jeffries finally stopped quivering, and his head dropped. Benny held on one more minute, then pulled his knife out, and let Mark Jeffries fall on top of an old gravestone. Benny breathed a deep sigh of relief. He had passed the test.

Benny took another drag from his cigarette and looked out the window. He had always felt guilty about killing Mark Jeffries but also knew he had followed the voice. Benny got up out of bed, poured himself a drink, and went into the bathtub. He wondered if he would ever hear the voice again, and he wondered why he had been chosen.

11 St. Boniface Cemetery

CHAPTER 7

A year or so after the night of the bar fight, Benny and Mary began to drift apart. Benny was getting a little bored with her. But he still paid for her apartment and would frequent it a few times a week. But things were changing between them, and they both knew it, but neither knew what it meant for their future.

One day, while walking along a busy downtown street, Benny accidentally knocked over a young woman. He helped her up, and he saw something in her. After apologizing profusely, Benny introduced himself. She told him her name too, it was Irene, and she was one of the 'good girls' in Chicago. For whatever reason, after meeting her, and taking her out on a couple of dates, Benny suddenly had a hard-on for settling down and starting a family.

Mary knew what was happening, she saw him with her a few times. She seriously considered stepping in to reassert her primacy in his life when she knew things were getting serious. But in her mind, she already had a good thing going, and she trusted her love for Benny would keep it going. Benny went ahead and got hitched, and to Mary's dismay, it significantly interrupted their love affair, bringing things to a stop for over three months. Mary began to fear it might be over. In her mind, she started making plans to move on, and would probably move out of the apartment. But Benny kept paying the rent, and that gave her hope.

One night, only three months into the marriage, Benny knocked on the door of Mary's apartment. It was a joyful, heartfelt reunion, and they made love for hours. Benny vowed to her that he would start coming as regularly as he was able to, and he did, seeing her now a once or twice a week.

Benny and Mary were falling deeper and deeper in love with each other. It seemed that the forced time away had only made their meetings that much more special. But on an evening in late July 1952 things changed again. Benny showed up at her door and knocked, his face held a wide smile that he could not erase if he tried.

Mary opened the door, "Hi Benny." She looked at him puzzled for a moment, "Why are you smiling like that?"

"Because I'm going to be a father. Can you believe that shit?"

The words pierced Mary's heart, everything inside her instantly knew what this meant. She tried to force a smile but turned away.

"What's wrong?" he asked.

She shook her head as she walked into the kitchen and nervously grabbed a cigarette. "Nothing's wrong Benny. Congratulations."

Benny went over to her and pulled her around hugging her tightly. "Hey, nothing gonna change between us. I love you, Mary."

She kept her head down and pushed him away. "I need to be alone."

"Mary, I told you, nothings gonna change."

She looked up with moistened eyes, "Look, I need to be alone right now. Now just get out of here."

Benny nodded and reluctantly left. As soon as she closed the door, a myriad of emotions fell upon her. Mary had her own deep desires of having a family someday. She wanted a family with Benny, but not right now, and suddenly it all seemed so far away. Mary cried for a long time and finally fell into bed exhausted and worn out.

April 8, 1953, Chicago... 8 months later

It was an unusually windy and cold night in April as Sister Joan walked at a frantic pace down the 4th-floor hallway of the Arthur Jones Memorial Maternity Hospital. She reached the stairwell and hustled down three flights of steps to the first floor where the hospital Chapel lay tucked at the end of the hall. Inside, her superior Sister Agnes was alone, kneeling before the Blessed Sacrament praying. Sister Joan went in, quickly genuflected, then walked directly to her.

Sister Joan leaned forward and whispered in her ear, "Mother, I am sorry to disturb you. There is a problem."

"What is it?" asked Agnes asked, keeping her head bowed and her eyes closed.

"It's one of the newborns. I am..."

Just then, a young man walked into the chapel and knelt in one of the back pews. Sister Agnes opened her eyes and signaled Sister Joan to come closer. She listened, as her eyes gradually widened. She swallowed and turned to her with a worried look on her face. She got up, her heart suddenly racing, genuflected, and followed Sister Joan back up to the 4th-floor ward.

They walked into the small room adjoining the viewing ward where parents could see their newly born babies. Two nuns were standing next to a table where the baby lay covered in a blanket. Sister Agnes looked at their faces as she approached. She could see the fear they held. She nodded to them, and one of them lifted the blanket while the other turned the boy over.

Sister Agnes's eyes narrowed. She pulled the light closer and bent down. There on the upper portion of the back of the boy's hip was the cloud shaped mole. There was no mistake, it was the mark, the Mark of Cain, and it was darker and more prominent than she had ever seen.

"What shall we do Mother?" Sister Joan asked as they all stared at the fussy infant.

Sister Agnes closed her eyes for a moment, trying to calm her racing heart. "I need time to think. Cover him up." With that, she turned and left, heading straight back to the Chapel.

Outside of the ward, Benny stood looking through hall window, scanning the room for his baby boy. He saw two nuns walk out of the room, followed by two more nuns cradling a little baby. They put the baby in a crib and hung a small sign that said, "Baby Boy Paddock." Benny smiled widely, watching them intently, as the two nuns covered the child, paused, and said a prayer before leaving.

Benny shook his head smiling ear to ear. Before him was his first born that he and Irene had decided to call Stephen.

Downstairs in the Chapel, Sister Agnes and Sister Joan knelt next to each other with their rosaries held tightly in their hands, praying fervently. They knew what the mark meant. They knew too, how dark it was, and because of this, they had a solemn duty. Sister Joan leaned over and whispered, "I don't remember it ever being that dark."

Sister Agnes kept her eyes fixed on the crucifix and nodded.

Sister Joan then said, "It seems that we must act."

Sister Agnes closed her eyes for a moment, and nodded again, saying, "Yes, we must. Do you remember the baby from 20 years ago?"

Sister Joan frowned, then nodded. She got up, genuflected for a long minute, then walked out of the chapel.

Sister Agnes started to get up, but stopped, suddenly remembering the child. Part of her never felt comfortable with it, it saddened her that the parents would never know the truth. But another part of her knew she had carried out the sacred duty passed down through the order for hundreds and hundreds of years, the duty to protect the world from the evil offspring. She knelt back down and began to pray.

Standing outside the ward, Benny looked in closer at the infant. He felt his anger building, anger he had not felt in a long time. It was the rage; it was back. He closed his eyes and took a slow deep breath. Suddenly he heard the dark voice, clearer than it had ever been. "Protect him, Benny, protect the child."

Just then he saw three nuns walk in. They went to the crib and bent over to pick up the child. Benny banged on the window loudly, startling them. "Leave him alone." Throughout the ward, babies began to stir and cry.

All three nuns were alarmed and froze. Benny pointed at them, then quickly walked around to the side door entrance to the viewing room. "I want him taken into his mother's room. I'm staying with him tonight, and we're going home tomorrow."

Sister Joan said, "Mr. Paddock, you are not allowed… "

"Shut up lady. I said bring him to her now." His voice sounded demonic.

Sister Joan tried to think of what to say, but Benny interrupted her thinking. "We are taking him to his mother's room, and I'm going with you. Now let's go."

Sister Joan stood frozen, knowing she had failed in her sacred duty. She slowly nodded and motioned for the other sisters to comply. Benny sat in a chair and stayed awake all night watching his little boy. He carefully oversaw every move the nuns made to care for Stephen during the night. In the morning, Benny packed up Irene and Stephen and left.

A few weeks later, on a dreary rainy Chicago evening, there was a knock at Benny's street-level apartment door. Benny was sitting by their small fireplace reading the newspaper. He looked out the window to see a man holding something in his hands. Benny could not tell who he was, so he got up, tucked his gun in the back of his pants and went to the door.

Benny opened the door, and a scowl came over his face. It was his father's old friend Mr. Miller. "What the hell are you doing here?"

Mr. Miller shook his head in disgust. "Is that all you can say?"

"I said, what the hell are you doing here?"

Mr. Miller now grimaced, "Before your father died, he gave me this box. He told me to make sure you got it."

Benny said, "He stopped being my father a long time ago."

Miller was a large man, as large as Benny was, and just as mean, even meaner if he wanted to be. He felt like kicking Benny's ass, but he knew what was in the box, he had read it all. He took a breath, trying to calm his anger, and said, "I heard you had a baby, so you need to see this. It has articles in it, and letters from your grandmother, and some other things you need to see."

"What the hell are you talking about?" asked Benny.

Mr. Miller said, "Look, your father insisted I give it to you, and tell you the box was your grandmother's, she gave it to him, and he wants me to give it to you."

Benny looked down at the old wooden box which was no larger than a shoebox. He took it, glared at Miller one more time, and slammed the door in his face.

Benny went inside, peering out the window, watching Mr. Miller get in his car and drive off. He heard Irene yelling from the back, "Who was at the door?"

"No one, just some guy selling stuff. He's gone now."

Benny opened the box and began to read about William Bury, and Dundee Prison, and Mrs. Marjory, and his own grandmother's letter, and letters from the lawmen of Dundee, Scotland. He sat there thinking, then said: "Jack the Ripper, the Mark of Cain, this is bullshit!"

He crammed everything back into the wooden box and tossed it into the fire.

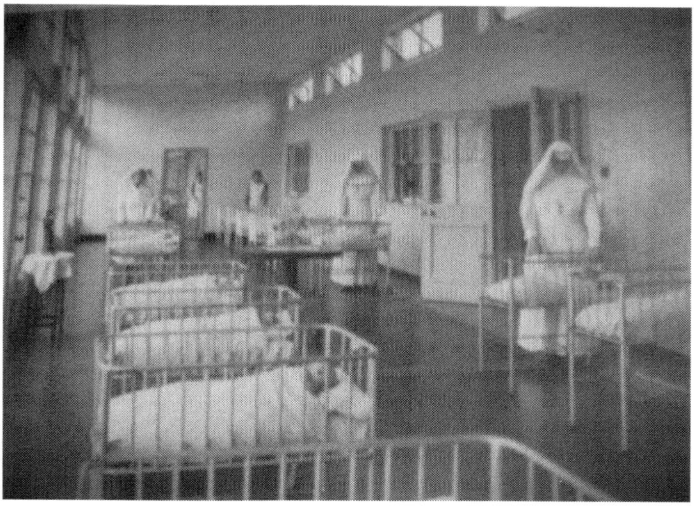

12 *Era Maternity Hospital*

CHAPTER 8

With the birth of Stephen things between Benny and Mary cooled for a long time. Mary took on other lovers, but none of them made her happy like Benny. When he did come over, all he talked about was his little boy, and Mary began to resent that. She also started to turn up her charms, and her wiles to bring Benny by more often. Within six months, things were getting back to how they used to be. Benny had told Irene he was now working as an out-of-town salesman, so he was free several nights a week. Irene was none the wiser, as Benny always brought home gifts 'from the road' and maintained a steady income.

It was life with Mary that Benny loved more than anything. On many hot summer nights, Benny and Mary would go out dancing at the Renaissance Blackstone, then have sex late into the night in one of their luxurious rooms. He hung out with Paul Rica's men during the day, taking care of business, occasionally pulling off a more important job, and spending nights with Mary.

Over the next several years Benny had two more kids with Irene. But he only continued to drift away. Irene and his family were his "on the side." Benny was falling deeper and deeper in love with Mary, and nothing mattered to either of them except each other, and their life of elegance supported by crime. But one night it all came crashing down.

It was 4:30 in the morning when Mary's phone rang. She answered, became confused, and handed it to Benny. "It's for you babe," she said, as she groggily rolled back over.

Benny sat up and took the call. "Yeah, who is this? Johnny, what the hell are you calling me at four in the damn morning for?" Benny paused, listening, "All right, go ahead."

As Benny listened, Mary sensed the importance and sat up. She watched him intently as a look of concern came over his face.

Benny shouted, "Dammit! Are you sure?" Benny paused, listening. "What does Mr. Ricca say?" He paused again, listening more carefully, then exclaimed, "Goddammit!" He got up and hung up the phone.

"Benny… what is it?"

He shook his head, grimacing, "I gotta leave town."

"What the hell are you talking about?"

"Looks like I got fingered by someone. The police are going to be looking for me, as soon as tomorrow." He was frantically picking up and putting on his clothes.

"What the hell happened?" Mary asked, panicked, sitting up covering herself with the sheet.

"We robbed a bank a few days ago, and one of our guys got shot. They caught him, and the word is, he's talking."

"What?" Mary said, as she threw the covers off and stood up. She nervously reached for her cigarettes. She knew she was about to lose the only man she ever truly loved.

Neither said a word, both of their minds racing. Then Mary asked, "Are you sure Benny? You gotta be sure if you're leaving town." She picked up a cigarette and quickly lit it, nervously taking a puff and promptly blowing out the smoke.

"I'm sure."

"Can't you stop him? Can't you do something? You got connections."

"They're working on it, but it's already happening. They don't have time, so I gotta get out of Chicago, now."

Mary's cigarette went out, and she nervously relit it, asking, "Where the hell are you gonna go?" He didn't answer right away. She took some long drags, slowly blowing out the smoke, wondering if there was another way, wondering if she should go with him. She looked around the room, thinking to herself, *nothing is holding me here.* She asked again, "Benny where are you gonna go?"

"I don't know. Maybe Tucson."

Mary suddenly felt hope, a courage welling up within her, "I want to go with you."

"No, I'm taking the family. I can't leave them."

"What the hell are you talking about? It's me you love!"

"I know that," he said in a frustrated tone, "but I can't leave them here, the boys are too young, especially Stephen."

"They'll be fine. You can send them money."

"No Mary… it's not time, but I'll find a way. I promise." He walked over to her and kissed her.

Mary was momentarily relieved. She really didn't want to uproot her life. She got up and held him tightly, as tears fell down her cheeks. She couldn't help but feel overwhelmed by their sudden goodbye. "I love you, Benny, I always will." They kissed once more, then Benny left.

CHAPTER 9

Benny drove home immediately. At 5:30 a.m. he pulled up to the front of his apartment and parked on the street. He saw his neighbor Bob Wiley look out his front window. "Screw you, Bob!" Benny said. He knew Bob couldn't hear him, but he hated him just the same. Bob was one of those people like Mr. Miller, and so was his nosey wife. Benny used them as examples of what *not* to be like in talks with Stephen.

He got out, shutting his Cadillac door loudly, and walked into his street-level front door.

He sat down in his living room, thinking of another way. After over an hour of agonizing thought, he finally woke Irene. "Irene, get up. I've made a decision."

The tone of his voice alarmed her. Irene bolted up, trying to shake off her sleep, "What are you talking about? What decision?"

"We gotta move to New Orleans. I gotta great opportunity there." He was lying about New Orleans. He didn't want any word of where he was going leaking out to any of her friends or their neighbors.

Irene asked, "New Orleans, when?"

"We're leaving today. Get the kids up and get packed. We won't need anything, I'm being paid lots of money to take this job. We'll buy everything new that we need once we get there."

Irene protested, "I can't just leave!"

Benny gritted his teeth and lowered his voice, "I don't think you heard me, Irene. We're leaving today, in a few hours, so get ready."

"But what will I tell the kids?"

"We can explain when we get there. Now let's go. I want to be on the road within a couple hours. I'll be back. Don't talk to anyone, don't tell anyone. Just get ready." Irene knew not to talk back to him when he was like this.

Suddenly she remembered her money, "Wait, what about my money?" Irene had inherited $4,500 from her father when he passed, and it was in a savings account at a local bank.

"We'll withdraw it before we leave."

Irene was beside herself, but there was little she could do. Her own parents were dead, and her siblings were not close to her. There was really no one to complain too. She had friends, but she was not close to them. With Benny's controlling ways and her taken care of three little kids by herself, she was busy and increasingly isolated.

Benny raced out to the south side of town, to the place where Paul Rica's men hung out. He explained his getaway plan and got paid early. He had more money stashed at home, but he was not going to miss out on his share, especially when he was being fingered for it.

When he got home, Stephen, now five, was in his room crying. Benny went in, "What's wrong Stephen?"

"I don't' want to go daddy."

Benny felt his pent-up anger burst forth. He grabbed Stephen and shook him. "Shut the hell up and get ready."

Stephen shuddered and watched his daddy leave the room. It was then that Stephen heard a small whisper for the first time, a dark whisper, in his mind. He felt his own anger rising, and he beat his fists into the pillow as the anger mounted. He ran into his little brother's room and pushed him down into the bed frame. His brother hit his head hard and started screaming, but Stephen only sighed with a small grin on his face and walked away, feeling better.

CHAPTER 10

The frazzled family lumbered down the highway in the '56 Cadillac convertible that Benny had bought the previous year. He loved that car and kept it clean, washing it and waxing it every Saturday morning before going down to the mob hangout. It had ample room in the back where Benny had his way with Ms. Mary on more than a few occasions. As he glanced back at his three boys in the back seat, a little part of him felt like Mary was coming with him. He snickered and kept his foot on the pedal, flying down Highway 55 heading south toward Tucson.

Irene felt strangely relieved. She had recently suspected Benny had been carrying on a double life, and now they were leaving the big city, heading to a new and exciting place in the South. She had long worried about her little boys being poorly influenced by the riffraff in their Chicago neighborhood. Perhaps this sudden move was an answer to her prayers.

Several hours into the trip, Irene pulled out the map. They were now well into Kansas, and she noticed they were not heading toward New Orleans. She looked over at Benny, "I thought you said we were going to New Orleans?"

"Yeah, there's been a change. That's where I was this morning. I had to make a choice, and they offered me more money to work in Arizona. I heard it's better, my contact told me it's the right move."

"What is going on Benny?" Irene suspected a lot of things about her husband, but she could ignore them more easily before this, as they made more sense.

"Look, I told you what's going on. Now why don't..." Benny paused, looking in the rearview mirror. Two of the boys were asleep, but Stephen was awake, looking out the window. Benny looked over at Irene and motioned to the back, "We'll talk about it later."

"No! I want to talk about it now." She sounded panicked.

"Look, I have a job, it's gonna pay really well, like a lot more. I'm getting us outta that city, and into a good place to raise the kids. What the hell else do you want from me?"

Irene shook her head and looked out the window. She was beginning to regret marrying Benjamin Paddock more and more. They drove all day and into the evening, stopping to eat at some drive-throughs along the way. Benny wanted to be careful not to be seen, in case any wanted bulletins had gone out over the wires.

It was nearly 11 at night when Benny pulled into the Howard Johnson Motel in Tucumcari, New Mexico. They made it there in 15 hours, and he was happy they made good time. Everyone was asleep as he drove around to the room he requested in the back of the lot. He carried the kids in and laid them down in the double bed. Then he helped Irene get settled. His adrenalin was pumping. In the darkness, he forced himself on her, quietly laying her before rolling over and falling asleep.

Benny was the first to wake the next morning. He decided to go out to a nearby restaurant for donuts and orange juice. As he was leaving, he saw Stephen sit up. Benny felt bad about scolding the boy the previous day, so he motioned for him to be quiet, and come with him.

They walked to the restaurant. On the way back, the warm sun beckoned them, and they sat on a nearby bench to dig into the donuts.

Neither said a word. After eating for a while, Stephen said, "I feel mad daddy."

"Why Stephen?"

"What about my friends?"

"You don't worry about them, I'll be your friend now. You and I are gonna have lots a time together."

"But why daddy, why do we have to move?" The words caught Benny off guard. Until now he had been in a frenzy; trying to piece together his plan, getting his money, and getting on the road. Suddenly he realized just what was happening. He was being punished, punished by them all. It felt like that day his old man kicked his ass out in the snow when the cops brought him home.

The rage came again, and he grabbed Stephen by the shoulders, half lifted him, and looked into his eyes. "It's because of bad people Stephen, government types, people who hate me though I'm a good man… people who think they're better than us."

Stephen glared right back, trying not to cry because he was being squeezed so hard, he asked in a strained voice, "Like Mr. and Mrs. Wiley?"

Benny's mind suddenly eased, "Yes, exactly like Mr. and Mrs. Wiley. I've told you how hateful they are to me. Don't you ever be like those patriotic assholes! You hear me, boy? They are our enemies! Do you understand me, boy?"

"Yes… I hate them too," Stephen answered, as Benny's grasp tightened.

Benny glared deeper into his son's eyes. "You got to mean it, Stephen, you got to mean it!"

Stephen felt the connection forming with his dad. Tears formed in his eyes. "I mean it, daddy."

Benny put him down. For the first time ever, he realized Stephen had the gift, the same gift he had. He had this sudden realization that Stephen needed protecting, from his mom, from the authorities, because the world would never understand him. The world would hang him like they did Benny's granddaddy, or they would beat the hell out of him like Benny's old man did to him.

Benny took a bite of his donut, and looked down, chewing, swallowing. "This is our secret now. I'm gonna teach you about all the people you can't trust. But Stephen, this is between me, and you. No one else can know what I'm teaching you. It's our secret. Do you understand? No one… not even mom. Is that clear?"

"Yes, daddy."

"Now wipe those tears off and act like a man."

CHAPTER 11

They returned to the motel room, and the family joined in breakfast. Benny then packed the boys into the car, slapped Irene on her ass to her loud complaint, and closed the door. He quickly went around to his side of the car and paused for a moment. A woman was staring at him from the hotel lobby window across the parking lot.

"Dammit!" he yelled.

"What's wrong Benjamin?" Irene said in a startled voice.

The woman looked away, and Benny realized he may have been a little too jumpy. But then she looked over again for another long moment, and he was suddenly not so sure. He casually got into the car and started the engine.

Irene asked again, "What's wrong?"

"Nothing's wrong, I just… never mind." He put the car in drive and slowly pulled out, going past the lobby, eyeing the woman who was now *not* looking. She turned to look again at them, then turned back to the clerk.

"Goddammit!" he said aloud.

"Benjamin!" cried Irene.

Benny shook his head with an evil grimace on his face. In his peripheral vision, he saw Irene still staring at him, wanting a response to her silent complaint of him using such language in front of the kids. He glanced into the mirror and saw Stephen staring at him with a strange look on his face as if trying to understand; no, trying to support his father. Benny winked at Stephen and smiled.

Stephen smiled back.

Irene burst out, "You're terrible! I don't want you swearing in front of the children! I mean it!"

"Or what?"

Irene closed her eyes, sighing, taking in a breath, trying to calm her spirit. It was no use arguing with Benjamin Paddock; he did whatever he wanted. Before she could open her eyes, she heard Stephen mutter from the back seat, "We won't have to see damn Mr. and Mrs. Wiley anymore, will we daddy?"

Irene grimaced and glared at Benny. She turned around and slapped Stephen on the head, "You shut your mouth. Where did you learn to talk like that?" She already knew where, and it killed her. She had never heard Stephen swear before, maybe little childish swear words, but not like that.

"Leave him alone!" said Benny.

Irene glared at Benny and said, "I'll talk to you later."

For the next hour, no one said a word. Finally, they stopped for gas and Benny got out to pay.

Irene looked in the back, "Stay right here." She got out and waited for Benny to come out of the store. As soon as he did, she demanded, "I need to talk with you."

"What do you want, Irene?" he replied with annoyance.

"I want you to stop talking like that in front of the children."

"Stephen knows what assholes those people were, and I'm not going to hide it from him."

"You are insane!" She hit Benny on the shoulder with her fist, trying to hurt him, but he only laughed it off. Then, he quickly raised his hand as if to strike her. Irene cowered, and he laughed again. He looked over at the car and saw Stephen watching them, with no feeling in his eyes.

Irene started to cry.

Benny told her, "Get back in the car."

When she got in, she covered her face, crying softly, struggling to stop after being so humiliated in front of her children.

Stephen saw everything, and he felt bad he had let his dad down. As Stephen listened to his mother crying, he vowed he would keep the secrets between him and his dad next time. He would never again let his mom know what they talked about.

Benny got back in the car and looked in the mirror again and saw Stephen staring out the window. Benny could see that his anger was growing, and he knew Stephen was going to be very special.

As they drove into the city limits of Tucson, Benny had three ideas working their way through his criminal mind. First, he was going to find a place for his family, but most importantly, for Stephen. Second, he was going to find a way to take advantage of the law in Tucson. He saw the deputy cars on his way in, they were no Chicago police, and they were no FBI men either. He started to imagine pulling off robberies without having to divvy up the loot with five other guys. Lastly, he needed to get Mary out there. He needed her body, he needed the inspiration she gave him, but mostly, he needed the excitement she created in his life.

CHAPTER 12

Benny rented a room at a small motel on the corner of Ochoa and Stone Avenues. After he got Irene and the kids inside, he announced, "I'm going out to get us some dinner."

"Why don't we just go out for dinner?" replied Irene.

"Because I have to do some things and find us a house to live in. Stay here like I said!" He glared at her, and went out, closing the door firmly behind him. He put on his hat and sunglasses and started walking north up S. Stone until he spotted Steinfeld's Department Store. *Steinfeld's? Damn Jew boys all the way out here!* He headed for the entrance then stopped. Across the street was the Pima County Sheriff Department. *Shit!* He paused and sat on a nearby bench for a while scoping it out. It looked like there was a shift change, as lots of regular cars were coming in, probably deputies reporting for work. Patrol cars were also coming in, possibly ending their shifts. Benny waited another 20 minutes until it quieted down, then crossed the street and walked around the block, entering Steinfeld's from the other direction.

He walked into the men's section of Steinfeld's, feeling like a big tough Chicago mobster. He found a pair of western looking pants, a plaid western shirt, and some cowboy boots. He put them on and topped it off with a cowboy hat and a thick leather belt. He looked in the mirror of the dressing room and began polishing his newly thought-of western accent. "Howdy there

Mr. Paddock. How do?" He laughed, went to the cash register with his old clothes in his hands and paid. He then went over to a nearby diner and picked up some dinner, along with the newspaper, and headed back to the motel.

As the family ate, Benny opened the paper and made some phone calls, telling the prospective landlords, in front of Irene, that he was in town for a new job and needed a home right away. By the fourth call, he landed a prospect. He stood up and announced, "I gotta go meet a man. I'll be back."

Irene protested, "Benny why are you leavin' us here?" She was tired of being cooped up the with kids so long.

Benny didn't reply. He knew she was upset, but if they were looking for him, they'd be looking for a family. He would go alone and get the lay of the land. He had to find a home for his family. Within the hour he met Mr. Carpens at a house on 1100 North Camino Miraflores in Tucson, just about 10 minutes outside of downtown.

The house was ample size and already furnished. The yard backed up to the foothills and was over an acre. But more importantly, there was a guest cottage in the back of the property. Benny rented the house on the spot, paying three months in advance. The willing landlord handed him the keys and told him he'd check up on them soon. Benny smiled and responded, "No need Mr. Carpens, we'll get on just fine. Just give me your phone number, and I'll call you if we need anything."

As they exchanged information, Benny asked him one more question: "Mr. Carpens, what time does it get dark around these parts?"

Carpens looked at his watch. "Oh, I'd say in about an hour and a half." Mr. Carpens pointed over to the west end of the property. "The sun sets over there, and that'll be in an hour."

"I figured, thanks."

Mr. Carpens drove off, and Benny found a corner pay phone to call the motel's front desk.

"I need to talk to the lady in room 9."

"Who is this?"

"This is her husband. I was just over there earlier, renting it from you."

"Just a minute." They brought Irene to the front desk to take the call.

"Irene, it's me. Don't say anything. Not even my name. I don't want people knowing our business, or even who we are till we get established. You got that?"

Irene was annoyed but compliant, "Where are you?"

"Look, never mind that. I found us a beautiful place. I just must wait here for the man to go get me the keys. I'll be by within an hour or so. I'll pick you up and bring you and the kids over here. We'll get some groceries, and we'll have a nice dinner together." Benny did not want to risk driving around town in the daylight just yet. Now that they were so close, he was feeling paranoid, very paranoid.

Irene said nothing.

Annoyed, Benny said, "All right, keep everyone safe in the room. I'll be there soon."

"Yes, fine." She hung up.

He walked back to the guest cottage. Mr. Carpens had told him it had been empty for several years. Benny looked around. It was dirty and dusty, but it would do. He looked up at the ceiling. There was a small opening for an overhead crawl space. He got on a chair and looked inside.

He smiled, then went out to his car, popped the trunk, and took out a few bags of bundled cash, including the one that held Irene's money from her father, and hid them in the crawl space.

He then went out on the back porch, smoking the remainder of a cigar he had, and watching the sunset. Once the sun was nearly down, he left to pick up Irene and the kids. As soon as they arrived at the house, the stir-crazy children burst out of the car, running all over in the twilight before nightfall. Irene looked around with a smile on her face.

She liked the place, finally seeing a small glimmer of hope. It was an exciting moment for everyone, as the cramped city apartment they had was suddenly replaced by a real home in the countryside just outside downtown Tucson.

One of the children ran to the guest cottage and opened the door. Benny shouted, "Hey, get out of there." He turned to Irene. "No one's allowed in there. That's my office."

Irene said, "Fine. I want to go into town tomorrow morning and open a bank account."

"No Irene, not now. I'm going to build a secret place in that cottage to hide the money. It's safer than in a bank anyway."

"Benny, I think…"

"Listen, Irene, you need to start trusting me. No bank accounts right now. I don't trust them. I'll hide the money tonight, and I'll show you where it is tomorrow."

She shook her head, her moment of solace spoiled, and went in to see what needed to be done to get everyone ready for dinner and bed.

CHAPTER 13

The family loved their first year of life in Tucson, especially the warm winter. It was a time of renewal for the family. Benny had more time to spend with Stephen, the time he never had back in Chicago. During this time, Benny took seriously his responsibility to teach and protect Stephen. The other boys did not matter to him as much. None of them had the gift he and Stephen shared.

It was July 4^{th,} 1958 when Benny packed Stephen and his two younger brothers into the back of the Cadillac convertible. He beeped the horn, and in a moment, Irene came running out of the house, holding a small bag with some drinks and snacks in it. They were on their way to the annual parade. They drove downtown and parked behind the Steinfeld's department store at the corner of Stone and Pennington Streets. Benny took the folding chairs from the trunk, and they walked over and set up to watch the parade.

As the parade began, Benny began to feel antsy. His anger at the government had abated some, being out of the city helped with that, but the sheriff and deputies hanging out all around the parade route began to bother him. It reminded him of why he was in that God forsaken city, and why he was not screwing Mary anymore. The high school marching band came down the street first, with signs and music, and a whole line-up of baton girls.

Then came the WWI, WWII and Korean War veterans. Benny heard the faint dark voice that always preceded his rage. The rage grew as now sailors passed by, just like the ones who screwed with him at Halligans. He felt the hatred for his father returning, the hatred he felt for them all. He thought, as he stood up, lifting Stephen, and stepped back a little so Irene could not hear him. He whispered into Stephen's ear, "It's because of assholes like these that we had to leave Chicago. Just remember, these guys are *not* our friends." Stephen didn't look away from the men but only nodded.

The Chamber of Commerce group passed by next, but it was also the one that set Benny off. There were lots of members walking on all sides of the float, carrying little American flags. Seeing all the patriotic flag-waving people unnerved Benny more than the sailors. He set Stephen down, took him by the hand, and said, "Stephen and I are gonna go get us all some hot dogs."

"All right, hurry back," remarked Irene, as she pulled both younger boys onto her lap.

Benny hustled down the lined street, pulling Stephen along to meet up with the approaching float. He had something to teach him. He picked him up, and moved to the front, finding a place in front of a lamp post. On top of the float was a country western singer. He was up there with his cowboy hat strumming his guitar and singing. Benny looked around at the crowd, all waving their flags, clapping along. He said quietly, "Stephen listen to me, look around at these flag-waving country assholes, they're not like us, you understand! They think they are better than us. These are people just like the Wiley's, you understand that, don't you boy?"

Stephen glared at them, nodding.

"Good," said Benny, "cause, I never want you to forget it, never forget what I showed you today."

As Benny turned around to go back, he bumped into a man in a cowboy hat. The man stepped aside politely, but Benny said under his breath, "get the hell outta my way."

The man shook his head and walked away, glaring at Benny as he did. Stephen watched the man eyeing his dad. Stephen now felt his rage grow. His little fist tightened as he turned to look at the man with gritted teeth.

The man saw Stephen and looked at him for a moment. He saw a coldness in Stephen's eyes that sent a shiver down his spine, he had never seen such coldness in a child's eyes.

13 ***4th of July Parade***

CHAPTER 14

By now it had been over a year since they arrived in Tucson, so Benny decided to make a few calls to find out what was happening in Chicago. Benny's former associates told him they heard that the Chicago Police were no longer searching for him. The rat who squealed ended up getting snatched up, chewed up, and mixed in with the garbage at the dump on Chicago's South Side before he could testify. The investigation had gone cold. It was safe for him to come back.

The thought occurred to Benny of returning, and he seriously thought about it for days after hearing the news. But the truth was, he loved his life in Tucson. Irene was happy, Stephen and the boys were happy, and Benny was beginning to get to know people.

In the spring of that year, Irene had her fourth child, another boy. It was a time of joy for the family, and it brought Benny closer to his family for a while. Since Mary was not around, he spent more and more time at home. He no longer had any reason to lie to Irene about staying away from home, so he informed her that he quit his sales job, and opened a small appliance shop downtown, selling a new product called a garbage disposal. He didn't give a damn about garbage disposals, but it gave him respectability in the community and a front with Irene.

One day, the new Pima County Chief Sheriff James W. Clark

wandered into the store. Benny's heart began to race. Perhaps his contacts were wrong, maybe Sheriff Clark was there to do some snooping around.

"Can I help you, sheriff?" Benny asked from behind his small cash register counter.

"Hi there. I heard about this place. I'm Sheriff Clark, James Clark."

Benny stuck out his hand, smiling, "Well how do you do Sheriff Clark. I am Benjamin Paddock, at your service."

Sheriff Clark took his hand, then paused, and took a double take, "Do I know you from somewhere?"

"I get that all the time, sheriff. My old man used to say I look like Curly from The Three Stooges, just a taller version."

Sheriff Clark burst out laughing, as the men shook hands.

Sheriff Clark wandered toward the display. "My wife wants me to get her one of these garbage things you got, what do ya say about them?"

Benny walked right over, stood next to the displays, and started his pitch, "Oh, they're wonderful, sheriff. My wife swears by ours. Most of my customers come back and tell me how much they like them." Benny was a born salesman.

"Well how much are they?" asked the sheriff.

"They sell for $27, but I'm gonna tell you what sheriff. I am a friend of law enforcement so I will give this to you for what it cost me."

Sheriff Clark graciously replied, "Oh, you don't have to do that."

"Oh, now Sheriff Clark, I insist. I lived a tough life when I was young. I like to give back every way that I can."

"Well, that sounds good. I'll take it."

Benny went into the back and picked up a new one. He took a deep breath. He was nervous as hell. He calmed himself down and went back out front with a smile. "That'll be $16.93, sheriff."

The sheriff paid him and thanked him. He was about to leave when he stopped and turned around, "You know Mr. Paddock, I'm forming a community program to help some of our youth, to get them on the straight and narrow road if you know what I mean. Would you be interested in helping us?"

"I don't see why not," Benny replied smiling, but inwardly cringing.

"Well there's a meeting tonight at the station at seven, I would be obliged if you could come."

Benny's mind was racing as to how he could get out of it politely. But in his mind, he was fumbling, there was no good excuse he could think of. "I would be honored, sheriff. I'll see you tonight."

That night Benny parked his car two blocks away, in case he had to make a getaway, and walked over to the Pima County Sheriff's Department on the opposite corner of Stone and Pennington, across from Steinfeld's. There were six other men in the lobby, all apparently there for the same meeting. Benny found it intriguing at how backward and calm the department looked compared to the sophisticated, chaotic environment of Chicago. He was within a mere few feet of more than twenty desks, all manned with men and women on phones, surrounded by maps of the area plastered all over the walls.

A deputy came out and greeted everyone and took them through the bullpen of activity into a conference room where they all filled out applications. Then Sheriff Clark came in and addressed them, telling them about the 10-week evening course.

They would receive special deputy status and be allowed to participate in several volunteer efforts, including search and rescue, which the sheriff promised was of great interest. But more than that, they would have the chance to make a positive difference in the lives of the youth. Benny had planned on bowing out, but as he listened, the wheels in his Chicago gangster mind began turning. He saw the opportunity, the opportunity to be his own inside man, to be close to the pulse of law enforcement.

Three months later, Benny's family sat in the second row of the little audience as he received his Special Deputy badge along with the other four members who stuck it out. Benny was proud and felt a sense of accomplishment that he was now on the inside. He looked at Irene smiling at him along with the other children, but Stephen was not smiling. He had a glaring look on his face that alarmed Benny. After they went home and got everyone settled, Benny sat in the living room with Irene. He knew he had something to do. He couldn't let Stephen think he was letting him down. He got up, "I'm gonna take Stephen into town for a ride."

"Why would you do that? It's 8:30 at night."

"Because I want to, that's why," Benny said stiffly. He went in and got Stephen out of bed and took him for a ride. They went into town and got an ice cream. Benny said, "Stephen listen to me, I want you to know what I'm doing'. But you need to promise me you'll never speak a word."

Stephen looked at him and slowly nodded. He did not tell his dad, but his rage had been simmering all night long.

Benny continued, "First of all," he paused, not sure where to start, "First of all, never let other people know what you're doing in life, or what you're going through. It's safer that way." Benny paused, watching his son take it in as he calmly licked his ice cream. "Now, you see this silly-ass badge I have." Stephen stopped and looked over at it, then continued licking his ice cream. Benny said, "You're probably wondering what I'm doing, joining these government assholes?"

Stephen half smiled at the swear word, amazed his dad could read his mind, then nodded.

"I'm getting' inside, Stephen. I'm gonna be able to know them, to know my enemies. If you can know your enemies, you can defeat your enemies. You understand?"

Stephen nodded again, he understood the secret part but was confused by the other. He began licking his ice cream cone again.

Benny patted him on the back, started the car, and drove home. He had Irene put Stephen into bed and went outside to think. The full moon was shining brightly, illuminating the backyard as he looked out from his porch. He realized he had come a long way. He had left Chicago, set his family up in a nice home on the outskirts of Tucson, become a volunteer deputy, and become a respectable businessman in the city.

But his money was getting low, and he never liked it when his money got low. He did not dare touch Irene's money. He had it hidden, and never let her up to see it, but she made him bring it out periodically and show it to her.

But this night, he found himself reminiscing about the old days, and it all brought him back to one thing, his beautiful days and wild nights spent with Mary. They were the happiest days of his life. He missed screwing her, he missed the way she made him feel, he missed everything about her. Somehow, with the stress of making sure Stephen would be protected, and keeping up his front, he had been able to turn her off in his mind, but tonight she came rushing back in.

Before him, shining in the moonlight was the little guest cottage, the cottage he had already set in his mind would be Mary's someday. He decided right then, it was time to bring her home.

14 Steinfeld's

15 Pima County Sheriff Badge

CHAPTER 15

On a warm February night Benny went into town to the telephone booth outside the Sears store. He went in, closed the booth door behind him, picked up the phone, and dialed the number. The operator came on and told him how much to deposit. He heard the phone ringing. He was excited to talk to her, and when he heard her say hello to the operator, he instantly knew he had made a mistake leaving her behind.

"Hello?" Mary said cautiously.

Benny blurted out, "Mary!"

"Benny?"

"Mary, oh Mary I miss you."

"Oh, I miss you too Benny."

There was silence.

He continued, "Mary I've thought about nothing but you every damn day since I had to leave."

Mary started to cry. "Why did you leave me here alone. I thought you were gone forever, Benny. Damn you for leaving me."

"I'm sorry Mary. I'm bringing you out here with me now. I need you, Mary, just like I always needed you. There isn't anyone else. There'll never be anyone else."

There was silence again. Finally, Mary said, "Benny, I've been thinking about you, don't you know that I love you."

"I love you too Mary. That's why I'm calling'. I want you to come out here."

"Come out there? What about your *wife*?"

"Don't worry about her. The boys are getting older, I told you I had to just get them settled. But I need your help. We're gonna make our own way out here. It's nice out west, you'll like it. No more damn snow, I'll tell ya that."

"Oh, that sounds good, but I don't know." Despite her words, Benny could hear the growing enthusiasm in her voice.

Mary asked, "What am I gonna do out their Benny?"

"You're gonna help me get set up out here. When we have enough money, we're gonna leave and go wherever the wind takes us, doll. Wherever you want."

"That sounds too good to be true Benny, don't be lying to me."

"I'm not lying', Mary, it's why I'm calling."

"But where am I gonna stay?"

"Well, you'll stay at a motel for a short while, then stay with me. I gotta little house here, and there's a small cottage out back. It'll be perfect."

"Benny, what about your family? I can't..."

"Hold it, this is the best part, I've thought it through. The cottage behind our property is a nice place, and I'll be able to get back there to get my hands on you. Besides, I still got the Cadillac, and it's nice and warm here all the time. But that's not why I'm bringing you. There are some jobs we can do down here. These country bumpkins don't know a thing about big city robbers. This is a big-ass area covering several states, we can pick and choose and take our time."

"But what the Hell are you gonna tell your wife?"

"I can tell her a lot of things. I'll tell her you're my old sales assistant from Chicago, and I've hired you to help me at the store. I'll tell her you're staying with us temporarily until you find a place of your own. But no matter what Irene says, that cottage in back is for you. I knew it the first moment I saw it."

"I don't know Benny. I want to but..."

"Look, I'm telling you, this is our chance! Now, will you come?"

There was silence on the line as Mary thought it through. Benny crossed his fingers hoping she'd say yes.

Mary finally gave him her answer. "Yes Benny, yes, I'll come."

Benny let out a yell! "I can't wait to get my hands on you, Mary."

"Me too Benny. It's been so long, me too."

"Pack it up and get on the Greyhound bus for Tucson. How soon can you come?"

"I can leave in three days."

"All right, Wednesday you get on the bus. I'll be checking the station starting Friday evening. I'll get things ready here."

"See you soon Benny, it's going to be just like old times."

"Yes, it is Mary, even better."

The next day Benny decided it would be good to create his own personal arsenal, it would help Mary to realize how serious he was about being his own boss. He remembered Mr. Touhy used to have one in Chicago. They would often have drinks with him and plan their jobs sitting in front of his gun case. Touhy would always walk over, and take one down, pretending to be aiming it while he listened and gave them instructions.

Benny went to a gun store in Tucson and purchased two rifles. He also bought another handgun, a more modern one than the snub-nosed pistol he had brought from Chicago. He took them back to his store, and in the back room, built a mounting wall, where he could display them. As soon as he finished hanging up the two rifles, along with the pistol, he knew he had to show Stephen. But he waited because he wanted to buy a few more.

The next day he looked up a different gun shop, further out of town. He went there, and bought two more rifles, along with two more different looking handguns. He brought them back to the store and mounted them. He then went to the hardware store and bought two small lamps, which he installed at the top of the mounts so he could turn them on.

When he was finished, he went home and got Stephen, bringing him back to the store. It was evening. "I got something' special to show you tonight Stephen, but you can't tell your momma or your brothers. Got that?"

"Yes, daddy. I do."

"Alright, come on back here." Benny walked into the back room. As soon as Stephen came in, he turned on the lamps. "How do you like these Stephen?"

Stephen looked up at the shiny new guns mounted on the wall. They looked really cool to him. He turned to his father, "I like them, daddy. Can I hold one?"

"Sure, you can."

Benny took down a rifle and made sure it was not loaded. He

handed it to Stephen, and let him try to hold it, and pretend to aim it. Stephen pointed it right at him. Benny laughed and took it from him. "Someday Stephen, when you get older, me and you are gonna do some special things with these guns."

Stephen smiled, and Benny turned off the lights and took him out for ice cream.

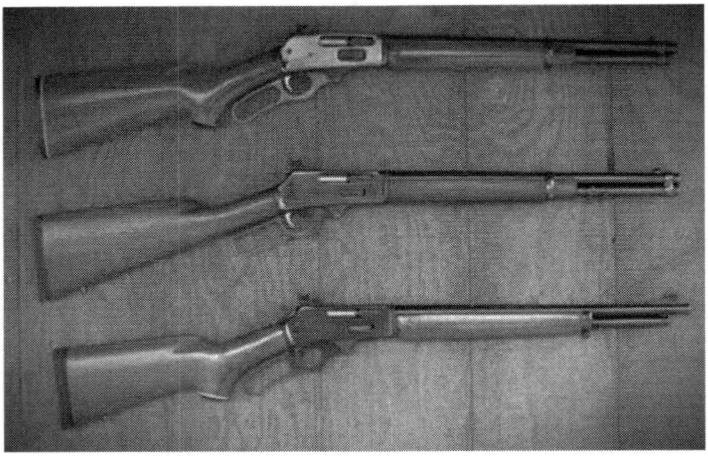

16 Benny's Wall of Guns

CHAPTER 16

That Friday night, Benny got up from watching television with Irene and announced, "I'm going into town."

"Where in town? It's Friday night, and it's raining out for God's sakes."

"I have something to do at the shop, and it can't wait."

Irene knew not to ask any more questions.

Benny grabbed his keys, put his hat and boots on, and went outside. He drove to the Greyhound station downtown. He'd already planned where to take her and rented a nice motel room that morning. He was getting a hard-on just thinking about getting his hands on Ms. Mary Jaycox. He looked at his watch, the bus was already 20 minutes late. He turned off the car and waited.

Finally, the bus pulled up and dropped several passengers at the front door. Benny waited for them to go inside, then he went into the tolerable rain and walked across the street. He looked in through the front window and scanned the people milling about in the terminal lobby. She wasn't there. He started worrying. He went back outside. The bus door was still open, and Benny could see a shadow of someone moving forward toward the front.

A little old lady with a cane appeared in the open doorway,

slowly making her way out. Then he saw someone behind her, reaching around to hold her steady while she turned the corner. Benny smiled, it was Mary.

Mary saw him, and the widest smile came over her face. She helped the lady down and over inside the terminal door. She then turned and ran to him.

"Mary!" Benny said as she dropped her suitcase and jumped into his arms. They embraced in a long loving embrace. Benny said, "You look so wonderful. C'mon, I don't want anyone to see us around here yet. I gotta place for tonight." Benny picked up her suitcase and took her by the hand. He opened the car door and helped her in. He barely got the car started as they started passionately kissing. They drove south of town for about 15 minutes to the Round Up Motel on East Benson Highway.

As they pulled in Mary took a deep sigh. She was so relieved to be back with him. She loved him and hardly remembered ever loving anyone else. She looked over at his strong face, then glanced out the window at the red motel sign glaring in the rain. She watched him slowly drive past all the cars down to the last room on the right. She felt her whole body getting ready as Benny pulled up to the room.

They went in, and within a minute their clothes were strewn about the motel floor. Several hours later they both sat up in bed with cigarettes in their hands, basking in the long-forgotten elation that used to be their world.

"Benny, I… I can't even tell you how happy I am." She took a deep cleansing drag from her cigarette and let her head fall back in ecstasy before slowly blowing the smoke up toward the ceiling.

Benny nodded and closed his eyes. Mary knew he was thinking and didn't interrupt. She closed her own eyes, enjoying her cigarette, feeling warmth all over her body. Neither said a word for a while. Mary finally broke the silence, "So what do you have planned for me out here Benny?"

"I'm not sure on all the particulars yet, but I gotta plan. Before I tell you, I need to show you something." He got up and put on his light blue faded boxer shorts and his tee shirt. He peered out the motel door and walked outside. He opened his glove compartment, took his deputy badge out, went back in, and threw it on the bed.

Mary picked it up, turned it around and looked at it. "What do you have this for?"

"It's my badge. I'm a Pima County Special Deputy."

"What the *hell* are you talking about Benny? You're lying to me!"

"You see it right there." He pointed to the inscription on the badge.

"Benny, I don't understand," she said as she traced the raised letters with her fingers.

"I signed up for some community volunteer bullshit. I help keep troubled youth… outta trouble."

"Benny why the hell would you be doing' this if you're gonna be your own boss down here?"

"Well, I kind of got sucked into it, by the old sheriff down here, Sheriff Clark." His eyes began to glisten, and a so did his smile. "But once I did, I realized that I got my foot in the door, I got my eyes on these bastards. Don't you see? I know what they know."

A broad smile replaced the look of confusion on Mary's face.

Benny sat on the bed and unfolded the other thing in his hand, a small map. "Look here Mary. You see this station here?"

"Where?"

"Here," he pointed to an area he had circled on the map. "It's a small town called Aja. We gotta substation there with only two patrol cars. Near the end of the month, there'll only be one on the day shift because one of the deputies has a surgery."

"Well why you telling me this?" asked Mary as she sat on the bed trying to piece things together.

"Cause I'm gonna be up there Tuesday morning." He plopped his finger down on top of another circle where he had also written Valley National Bank. Mary looked closer. It was on Indian School Road up in Phoenix.

Mary started to smile again. "You're gonna rob that bank? How far is Phoenix?"

"It's a couple hours, and yeah, I'm gonna rob that bank. They just built it two years ago. I've already been up there a few times to scout it out. It looks like an easy job. It's right near Highway 51."

He laid out the map and knelt on the floor, tracing it with his finger. "I'm gonna park my car up here, by Desert View Village, steal a car from a factory over by here." He slid his finger slowly across the map. "Then, around 9 a.m. when it opens, I'll rob the bank. There's only one old man security guard I gotta worry about."

"Then I'll head north up 51." He traced the route with his finger. "I figure even if someone sees me, they'll think I'm heading north into the National Forest. I'll switch cars, and head south to Route 85 back into Pima County. See here, that's the Ajo substation I told you about. We'll drive right past it to Highway 86." He smiled and tapped on the map. "From there we drive right through the Tohona Indian Reservation back into Tucson."

Mary's eyes widened, "You got this all thought through."

"Yeah, I'm estimating I'll get about $5,000, maybe more."

"Who's going with you?"

"No one. I'm doing it alone. It's better, there'll be no more middlemen. It's all for me and you, Mary."

"I'm coming with you."

"Hell no," he responded.

"Oh, hell yes I am. It'll be better for you on those roads not to look like a single man. It'll be better if we look like a couple to throw them off." She took a quick drag and blew the smoke into the air.

Benny thought for a moment. He smiled, "You really wanna come?"

"Hell yes, what do you think I left Chicago for?" She puffed her cigarette again, this time blowing it out fast, and smiling, "This is our life now."

Benny smiled, nodding, "Like some modern-day Bonnie and Clyde."

"I like that Benny, just like Bonnie and Clyde." She put out her cigarette and knelt on the bed, letting the sheet that covered her fall by the wayside. "Now get over here and screw me again before I go crazy."

Benny kept Mary at the motel for a few weeks. He visited every day at lunchtime, closing his shop, bringing her lunch, and getting his just desserts.

A week before the robbery they drove up to Desert View Village to give Mary the lay of the land. They went around the area for a little while, then drove to the unguarded factory parking lot. He then took her to a small business district on Deer Valley Drive. "See that parking lot? I figure you can park there and wait for me. You'll see me pull in, nice and easy, and you'll wait till you see I parked. Then drive over by there and pick me up." He pointed to a spot behind the building. "You're gonna be driving. It'll look less suspicious."

Mary nodded.

They then drove down Highway 51, to exit 3 for Indian School Road. Within 4 minutes, 4 long minutes, they spotted the eagle-winged sign of Valley National Bank. The wings frightened Mary, though she didn't say anything. The giant eagle wings pointing outward gave them a military look that scared her.

"There it is," said Benny.

They pulled across the street and watched until it opened. They saw the old man security guard with white crew-cut hair and a cap open the door and unlock it. "Look at that old geezer."

"You're not gonna hurt him, are you Benny?"

"Naaa, not unless he pulls some hero bullshit. First thing I'm gonna do is have him slide his gun to me. It's better to be wanted for robbery than for murder."

Mary nodded; she was getting scared now hearing all these terms, "wanted," "robbery," "murder." But she said nothing and started fidgeting in her purse for a cigarette.

The next day Mary insisted Benny buy a family car to use for the getaway. He went out and purchased a nice-looking used blue Pontiac Bonneville Station Wagon. The boys loved it. Irene loved it and thanked Benny profusely. He accepted Irene's accolades and everything else that came with it. But it wasn't for her, or for them. It was for Mary.

Finally, the day came, and they left at 5:30 a.m. They made their way up to Desert village, got some breakfast nearby, and went over everything once more. As planned, Benny easily stole a car from the factory and drove it into the parking lot, waving goodbye to Mary, it was 8:25. The bank robbery went off without a hitch, and an hour later, at 9:20, Mary watched the stolen car slowly pull into the parking lot. He went over to the side of the building and parked. Benny got out carrying a large satchel. Mary smiled and picked him up.

Benny said, "Pull around back."

She did, he jumped out and opened the trunk. He carefully unhooked the carpet, rolled it back, and opened a concealed space he had made in the floor of the wagon. He put the money in, closed it, rolled back the carpet and hooked it into place. "Let's go. Head over there, go west."

Two and a half hours later, they had passed through the reservation and were back at the motel. They went in and checked everything out. Then Benny got the satchel and put it in the room. "You stay here. I'm taking the car home."

He did, and when he returned they counted the money together. There was over $11,000. "Oh my God Benny, $11,000! We're rich."

"Yeah, and that's just the start."

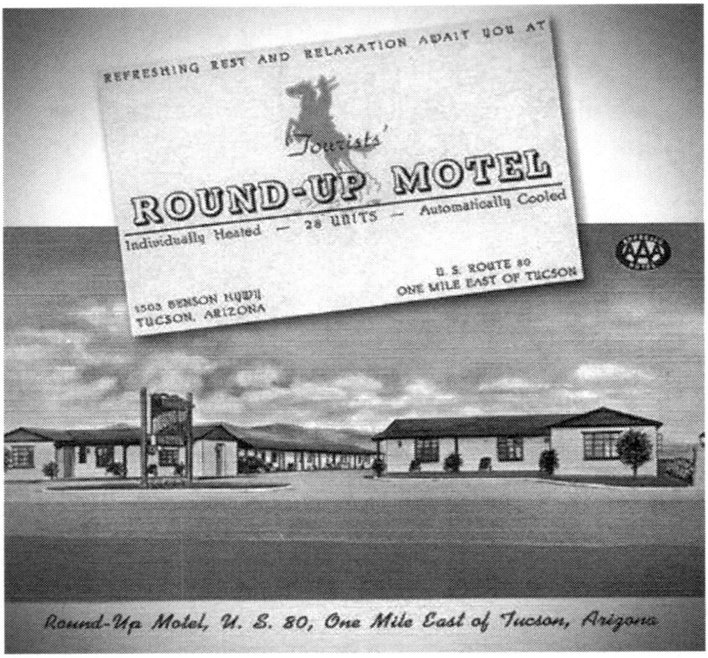

17 *Round Up Motel*

18 *Valley National Bank in Phoenix*

CHAPTER 17

The morning after the robbery, The Dark Angel Thaddus with his strong black wings glistening in the morning sun, flew toward the foothills surrounding Tucson. He had been summoned by the Dark Lord Legion. As he neared the meeting place, he began to feel anxious. Almost every Dark Angel feared Legion, and more than that, they tried their best to stay off his radar. Legion was fierce looking, and unfeeling, evil beyond all doubt. Being pulled in, or summoned by him only meant trouble, and for some, enslavement, or even death.

Finally, he spotted Legion standing ominously on a hillside overlooking Benny's house. Thaddus flew down, landed, and took a slight bow. "Greetings Legion."

"Thaddus," Legion said, with no emotion, "So, what is happening with your client, Benjamin?"

Thaddus pretended to be stumped and shrugged his shoulders. "I don't see anything unusual. He's a criminal, but not more than a low-level one. He's robbed a couple banks in his life, he hates authority, he hates people if you ask me."

"Does he have the mark?" Legion asked as an evil smile slipped from his dark lips.

The mere question immediately raised the tension of the conversation. Thaddus had the mark. All the Dark Angels bore it, for most it was faint, for some it was more prominent. Legion smirked impatiently, "Well does he have it?"

Thaddus shook out of his daydream. "I've... never checked. His father Mason did not have it, so I never bothered."

"Well find out! There is a draw on my power coming from here, and I need to know how important it is."

"I will, right away." Thaddus did not need one more thing to do, but that was not what was worrying him. He knew that Benny's grandfather William bore the Mark of Cain. But once it did not transfer down to his son, Mason, all worry about it being in the family line faded. The mark had never been known to skip a generation.

The next morning Thaddus arrived back in Tucson and went into the Paddock home. While he was waiting for them to wake, he thought back to Benny's grandfather, William Bury. Thaddus remembered well the 12 murders in Whitechapel London right before they hanged him. The remembrance of this fact comforted him, and he concluded in his mind that there would be none. The mark did not invent low-level criminals like Benny; it made monsters.

He sat in the living room until he heard the shower water go on. He slipped into the bathroom and peeked into the shower. It was Irene. Thaddus smiled and watched her shower for a few moments. She was a beautiful woman, there was no doubt. He wondered why Benny needed more. He went back to the living room to wait.

Irene came out and into the kitchen in a short pink robe with a towel wrapped around her head. Like most Dark Angels, Thaddus admired the women of earth. He watched her gracefully go about her duties. Suddenly he heard the shower water go on again. He sighed and went back into the bathroom.

Before him in the shower was a huge man. Benjamin was almost 240 lbs, and at 6′4″, he took up nearly the entire shower. Thaddus carefully scanned his body looking for the mark. Then he saw it, located just above the hip line on his lower back. It was there, but it was also slightly faded as if the top half was only partially there. Still, it was the mark, the Mark of Cain. His heart began to race, Legion would not be pleased that he had missed this. His only possible excuse was that it was partial, and perhaps insignificant. *But why is Legion's power being drawn from here?*

Thaddus was confused, he began muttering to himself, "We've never seen the mark skip a generation. What does this possibly mean? I know what it means, it means trouble for me."

He was about to leave when he heard a moan, then a voice from the back bedroom. "No… stop it! "

Thaddus turned, making his way down the hall. He opened the door to the boys' bedroom. It was the oldest boy Stephen, having some sort of nightmare. Thaddus half-smiled, and turned to leave, but for some reason stopped. He walked over and looked down at the boy. He said to himself, "You're wasting your time." He lifted the boy's shirt and inspected the left hip, where Benjamin had his mark. Thaddus eyes widened. There, in almost the same spot as the father, was the Mark of Cain, only this one was more prominent, very prominent.

"It can't be!" said Thaddus, starting down at the darkest mark he had ever seen. "I need to tell Legion, right away." In a panic, he turned to leave, but then looked back over his shoulder at the sleeping boy. Then he stopped. "Wait, I don't have to tell Legion. It will only put the spotlight on me, pressure I don't need. I'll tell him about Benny, but that's it." Thaddus sighed, relieved he had come to this conclusion, and left.

CHAPTER 18

Only two weeks after the robbery, Benny was itching for more. He rose extra early one morning and headed straight to the motel. He walked into Mary sitting up against the headboard in her bra and panties reading a newspaper. Benny announced, "We're doing' another job."

Mary sprung up on her elbow. "Why so soon? We haven't even started spending the money yet."

"Because they're not expecting it. I heard some of the deputies talking last night when I was at our meeting. They consulted this FBI agent on the phone, and he told them it was probably an isolated robbery. If there is going to be more, they will be a while, and some pattern will emerge. But no one expects anything now."

Mary felt nervous. "I don't know about this Benny."

"Look, I got it all figured out. It's gonna be even tighter than the last one." He grabbed his map from the table and spread it out. "Right here. I picked this one cause it's another new bank. They built it in '56, so it should be laid out similar."

Mary was feeling more afraid now. "I know Benny you got it all planned out… but I don't know about this. Can't we wait?"

"We will wait, after this job. Now let's go."

"Where we goin'?"

"We're gonna take a drive up there and scope everything out."

Mary got dressed, and they drove up to Phoenix, past the bank, then returned home along the getaway route. They decided the heist would be done the following Friday.

When the day came, they left early for Phoenix. The robbery was pulled off flawlessly by Benny, he used his salesman skills to 'sell the fear' by waving his gun around. The crowd inside the bank was petrified, and no one even followed Benny out. It was as if he merely went in and made a regular withdrawal and left. He met Mary, and they swapped cars. By the time they got back to the hotel, it was already dark. They counted the cash, there was $6,700. They were now sitting on over $18,000 from just two robberies.

They were too excited to do anything except make love; afterward, they fell asleep. The next morning, Mary woke up, threw on a sheer robe, and fired up a cigarette. Her body ached, but it was a good ache. Benny was twice her size, and he pounded her hard this time. She blew the smoke out into the room air and thought about the robbery. She couldn't believe how easy it had been.

Benny woke, lifting his head with a smile on his face, "What a day!"

Mary smiled too and took another drag of her cigarette, and asked, "How long do I have to stay in this God-forsaken motel?"

"I told you, you're gonna live in the back cottage at our house."

"Will that be any better than this?"

"Give me a week or two. I gotta get a plumber over there, and a painter, and make it really nice for you."

"All right, sounds good, just don't be takin too long."

"I told you, Mary, you and I are gonna build our life out here."

"Oh, yeah," she said, crushing her cigarette in the ashtray. "What about that family of yours?"

"They're getting older, especially Stephen, that little shit is just like me."

Mary wondered why he was telling her about his son Stephen. She didn't care about his family, she just wanted him all to herself. She asked, "What do you mean they're getting older?"

"What I mean is, when I'm sure Irene can handle the boys by herself, I'll leave her some money, and we'll take Stephen with us."

"And why the hell would we take Stephen with us?"

Benny felt his anger flare, "He needs me, Mary, I have to protect him. Besides, what the hell is it to you?"

"No offense Benny, but if I wanted a damn family, I'd have made my own. Someday I do want one, but with you, and whatever kids we have together. Stephen will be fine with his mom."

Benny glared at her, shaking his head.

Mary put her arms around his neck, kissing him, calming him, pulling him back into bed.

CHAPTER 19

A few days later Benny walked into the motel room unannounced and said, "We're going to a country concert up in Phoenix in a few days."

Mary replied, "A country concert, why the hell would we go to a country concert?"

"Cause, I got some tickets from one of the boys at the sheriff's department. I got three of them, and besides, I want you and I to scope something out up there."

"Well, who else are we takin'?"

"We'll take Stephen, I gotta thing or two to teach him."

Mary sighed, she was not happy, but she didn't feel like arguing.

On the day of the concert, Benny told Irene during breakfast, "A customer gave me an adult ticket and a child's ticket to a country concert up in Phoenix tonight. I decided I'll take Stephen up there, get us a little one-on-one time."

"Now why would you do that? He doesn't like country music."

"He'll be fine. Besides, I don't want to go alone."

"All right fine, take Stephen, but you better watch him, he's only 11."

That afternoon Benny and Stephen left at 3 p.m. They drove into town and pulled up in front of the Round Up Motel. Stephen looked at his dad with a question on his face. Benny smiled, "Stephen, we are picking up my assistant. She works with me at the store. But you can't tell mom because she'll get mad."

Stephen smiled and nodded. He was glad he and his dad had another secret between them. Benny jumped out and knocked on the door. In a moment, Stephen laid eyes on Mary Jaycox for the first time. He thought she looked pretty, but when he saw the way his dad catered to her every move, he began to dislike her. He instinctively got in the back seat and stared out the window most of the way up to Phoenix.

The concert was being held in an open-air stadium that was often used for rodeos. It reminded Stephen of the parade float his dad told him about. There were men and women all over wearing cowboy hats and boots, many waving little American flags. When the music started, it sounded too loud to Stephen, and it only got worse with people clapping and stomping their feet. Stephen felt his anger growing. All his daddy's teaching about who their enemies were was bothering him. Stephen looked over at Mary and saw her carrying on like the others. It only cemented it in his mind that she was his enemy, too.

At one point during the concert, Mary told Benny she had to go to the ladies' room. Benny nodded and took Stephen by the hand. He carefully folded his jacket with his gun in the pocket and carried it over his arm. They all walked down to the concourse together. Benny looked around and pointed to the left, "It's down that way, Mary. I'm gonna get us something to eat, and we'll meet you back right here."

Stephen watched Mary walk away, then his dad nudged him, "Let's go down this way and grab some food."

They walked down the dirt thoroughfare covered with straw. When they reached a concession stand there was a man selling popcorn and soda pop. Benny and Stephen arrived just as a couple of cowboys and their two sons also arrived. Benny put his arm in front of the cowboys, "We were here first."

"Oh, is that right?" said the one who looked at the other and then down at his boys. They all laughed.

It would have been over, except Benny said, "Yeah cowboy, that's damn right, you got a problem?"

"Now look mister, there isn't no need for that."

Benny shot back, "Screw you, you country lovin' son of a bitch."

The taller cowboy hauled off and punched Benny square in the jaw. It didn't faze him though, and he punched right back, knocking the taller cowboy to the ground. The other cowboy jumped in and leveled a hook right into Benny's temple. This time, Benny fell and skidded into the dirt, dropping the jacket he was carrying on the ground. Stephen felt his rage growing; he felt his fists tightening. He ran up, slugging one of the boys, shouting, "Get off him!"

Both boys turned on Stephen, knocking him down, pushing his face into the dirty straw, wailing on the back of his head. Stephen screamed, then got up. Out of the corner of his eye, Stephen saw his dad's jacket with the gun sticking out of the pocket. He looked over at the men, wailing on his dad. Stephen ran over to the jacket and picked it up, he reached into the pocket and began to pull out the gun. Just then Mary ran up and grabbed Stephen, taking the gun and jacket. She screamed at the men wailing on Benny, and they stopped and walked away. Mary quickly helped Benny up and paused to glare at Stephen for even thinking of pulling out the gun.

She ushered Benny toward the exit and snapped at Stephen to follow. Once they got outside, away from danger, Mary glared at Stephen again, then attended to Benny's injuries. "Benny, darling, are you alright?" She was crying, hugging him, wiping his face with a handkerchief. Benny took it all in, letting her pity him, he liked when Mary gave him such attention.

Stephen felt strange watching them; his anger toward Mary was growing.

"Let's go," said Benny, as they got in the car and drove off.

They stopped at a filling station, borrowing a wet towel to help clean up. Benny wiped the blood and dirt from his face, and yelled through his teeth, "Those goddamn country bastards. They think they're better than me. I'll show them someday."

Stephen felt happy, it didn't matter that his daddy was flaring up. Being in a fight with his dad had done something for him, it had released the rage into a smooth river of dark peace. He relished the moment, ignoring his daddy and his girlfriend. But he wished Mary had not stopped him, he wanted to shoot them.

As they drove, Benny turned to the backseat, "You did good son. You helped me against them country assholes. You did right." Benny sat back staring out at the highway while Mary nervously drove toward Tucson. His field trip with Stephen had gone better than he ever could have planned.

It was a dark baptism for Stephen, and his body felt it. All the way home, there was a burning, searing pain in the back of his hip. He tried to scratch it, but he couldn't see it. It was the Mark of Cain flaring. All the way home only one thing was going through his mind: His daddy was right, these people were his enemies, and so was Ms. Mary Jaycox.

19 *Country Boys in Phoenix*

CHAPTER 20

The following evening after dinner, Benny informed Irene that the woman he hired to help out at the store needed a place to stay, and she was willing to rent their little cottage. Irene initially objected until Benny pointed out her rent would practically pay for their own rent. Within two days, he had a plumber and painter over, and within a week the place was ready. Mary moved in, pulling up in a used car pulling a rented trailer full of new furniture and house apparels Benny had bought for her, including a color capable television.

Irene never spoke much with Mary, except to say 'hi' and 'goodbye.' Mary kept to herself when she was not working at the store. Irene knew there was more to the story, she just didn't know how much more.

As the months went by into fall, Irene began to take notice of Benny's nighttime excursions. She would hear him get out of bed, while she pretended to be asleep. Irene would then watch from the bedroom window as Benny's lumbering frame made its way to visit Mary in the back cottage. She felt desperate at first and shed a few tears of self-pity, but eventually, her thinking on the matter began to change. She needed to leave him, but there was a problem. He had whatever money they owned, and he had her money. Her options were very limited. Her parents were dead, but she had family in Chicago. She could go back there, perhaps meet someone who would fall in love with her, and marry her, even though she had four boys. She realized all she could do was bide her time and try to figure out a plan.

Meanwhile, Irene was no longer interested in pleasing him, especially with her body, and she considered telling him that. But she knew his violent side, and it scared her. She decided she would learn how to shoot their rifle. There were a couple of women at the school who knew how to shoot; she would ask them to show her.

But Irene was not the only person who saw Benny heading back to Mary's cottage each night. Many nights Stephen would lay awake in bed and hear the back door open. He would sit up in his bed on his elbow and watch his dad go back, and not come out for hours later. Stephen knew that Mary was upsetting his mom, and he knew she was hurting his family. His hatred for her began to grow.

Thaddus flew high in the sky, making his way to Arizona to officially check up on Benjamin, and unofficially, check on Stephen. He was still surprised they both bore the mark. Thaddus had no intention of being pinned down by two humans with the Mark of Cain. He had told Legion about Benny only because he had to, but he left out any mention of Stephen's dark mark. He did not want to be associated with someone whose crimes were purely evil. Dark Angel or not, he feared the Lord's wrath.

Throughout the thousands of years of human existence, when Dark Angels pushed their assigned humans too far, causing them to do unspeakable evils, they were given special punishment by the Lords and were put into Dark Cages for decades. Because of the freedom inherent in their nature, Angels of both sides feared Dark Cages more than anything.

Hundreds of Dark Angels suffered these punishments. Thaddus knew many of them deserved it for pushing people like Caligula, Chiang Kai-Shek, Hitler, Stalin, Ho Chi Min. All those monsters of humanity had one thing in common: They bore the mark and put it into full murderous action.

There were lesser actors too, followers usually, and their Dark Angels were also punished, though to a lesser degree. There had been over 60 Dark Angels who were involved with men directly part of Hitler's and Stalin's inner circles. After the war, they were rounded up, and to this day, a fair number of them were still locked up in those Dark Cages.

But to Thaddus the injustice was that even if the Dark Angel did not push his client to the extreme edge of evil, he was guilty simply by association, guilty by assignment. And some Dark Angels did not deserve what they got, because evil seemed to take over and there was little anyone could do. Thaddus knew he had walked a tightrope getting William Bury into Hell without being noticed by the Lords. But with Benny and Stephen both having the mark, he now had his hands full. He had to play his cards just right.

When he arrived, he went into the house to look for the boy. Stephen was playing with his brothers in the basement. Thaddus watched for a long while, trying to see, trying to understand what might happen someday. But there were no clues, except one. Stephen was very quiet, and Thaddus knew the quiet ones could be the most explosive.

20 *Dark Cage*

CHAPTER 21

One evening Benny noticed Stephen running back from the desert foothills behind the property. He didn't give it a whole lot of thought. A week later, he saw Stephen going back again. He stopped him, "Whatcha doing back up in them hills boy?"

"Nothing special daddy. I'm just playing,"

"Well don't be up there too long. I don't want to worry your momma."

"All right daddy."

Benny watched him run into the yard, past the cottage and up into the foothills. He smiled. He loved Stephen and was gonna make sure he grew up right.

A few days later, Benny saw Stephen going up toward the hills again, carrying something in his hands. He decided to give him some lead time, then follow him. After a while of walking, he saw Stephen kneeling in the dirt fidgeting with something. Benny paused, trying to see what he was doing. He walked up closer, trying to make it out, then suddenly stopped while his heart began beating fast. Stephen was kneeling before a dead bloody cat, which was mounted upon two steel skewer rods.

Benny froze. It had been so long ago. Then came the voice, the soothing voice he had not heard in so very long. Oh, but he remembered. He listened, carefully. *No Benny. Stephen is special. He is like you.*

Benny said, "Hey Stephen, what are you doing'?"

"Hi daddy," said Stephen, quickly standing, holding the knife behind his back.

"Did you crucify that cat?"

Stephen looked over at it, then back up at his daddy. "Yes, daddy."

Benny swallowed, then said, "I did that too when I was your age."

Stephen smiled, feeling proud, and pointed, "I did those too."

Benny felt shocked at his words as he looked to where he was pointing, but he would not let his face show it. Twenty feet away, just behind some rocks, was another one. It looked like it had been there at least for month or so. Benny took his son by the hand and walked over toward it. Flies were buzzing all around it. Before they got up close, Benny saw another. He scanned the whole area now, but there were only the three. He shook his head, remembering what his daddy did to him so long ago. He knelt, "Tell me, why did you do this Stephen?"

"I was angry daddy."

Benny knew the anger, and he also knew the voice.

"But why did you do that to it?" Benny asked gently, not wanting to alarm the boy.

"I heard a voice in my dreams telling me to. "

Benny felt a shiver go up his spine. "Stephen, I know the voice. I've heard it too when I was little. It's nothing' to be ashamed of boy." Benny knew he had to warn Stephen though, lest Irene see him. "Stephen, I need to warn you that... "He was interrupted.

"Benny? Stephen? What is this? What the hell is goin' on back here?"

It was Irene, she was walking up toward them, with one of the cats in plain sight. Benny got up and took Stephen by the hand. "It's nothing, Irene. Stephen's just playing' a game that all boys have played before. I did this too when I was a boy."

Irene screamed in a panicked voice, "Did you do this Stephen?"

Stephen looked up at her with a hint of a smile on his face.

Irene started yelling at Benny, "What are you teaching him?"

Benny let her go on for a few moments, he could not blame her for the shock. He grabbed her arms, "Stop screaming Irene!"

Benny looked at Stephen and snapped, "Get out of here." He then hugged Irene tightly, "Look Irene. I'll talk to him. He's just a kid, playing a dumb kid's game. I'll bury them cats and make him promise he won't do it again."

Irene was enraged, she looked at the cat again, and turned to Benny with a look of horror on her face. "This is sick! This... this is from the Devil, I know it!"

"Irene, that's enough, now get back in the house." He turned, guiding her back to the house. As they passed the cottage she stopped, Irene shrugged him off and said, "We have to take him to the doctor."

"No! No doctors! Now I told you I'll talk to him. Hell, one of his friends probably put him up to it."

Irene snapped back, "He doesn't have any friends!"

Benny now lost his cool, "Shut the hell up and get in the house."

Irene stomped off, crying and shaking.

Mary had been listening from inside the cottage. She walked outside around the back, and up the hill, seeing what they were so mad about. "Oh, my God." Mary was not religious, but she quickly made the sign of the cross and began to gag, throwing her hand over her mouth, trying to stop herself. Horrified by the evil display she saw, she walked back into the cottage, vowing to herself to find a way to get Benny away from Stephen for good. He scared the hell out of her.

CHAPTER 22

Some months later, on a hot summer day, Benny found himself at the sheriff's station for a special luncheon for the volunteer deputies. At lunchtime, Benny stepped out of the lunchroom and called over to the shop.

Mary answered the phone, "May I help you?"

"Mary, it's Benny. Can you bring over a boxed version of our latest model? Our new sheriff, Sheriff Burr, wants to buy one for his wife."

"Sure Benny, I'll be over in about 15 minutes. I'm gonna walk and get some air."

"Alright."

Mary was excited as well as nervous. She had never been inside the Sheriff's station, nor any police station for that matter. She grabbed the box, but at the last minute decided to drive. She parked and went in. A friendly deputy sitting at the counter greeted her and said, "May I help you?"

"Oh, hi, yes." Mary smiled, hiding her nervousness, "I'm dropping this off for Benjamin Paddock." She lifted the box.

The deputy said, "I know Benny, he's in the luncheon." He glanced over his shoulder into a conference room window. "Can you wait a few minutes; Sheriff Burr is handing out the awards right now."

"Oh sure. I'll just wait over here." Mary sat down in the empty waiting room and put the box on the seat next to her. There were some plaques on the wall that peaked her interest, so she got up and went over to look at them. They were historical accounts of the history of the Pima County Sheriff's Department. Mary was surprised at how many interesting photos of crime scenes, past sheriffs and deputies that there were.

Her eyes were drawn to what looked like an interesting case and began to read. It was about a young girl who was 7 years old. June Robles was her name, and she had been kidnapped and buried alive in a cage in the desert. Mary read anxiously, relieved to find they found her alive. She shuddered, *Oh my God. Buried alive!*

Mary moved over and read the next plaque. The title of the picture read, "The Hanging of Eva Dugan." Mary gasped. This old woman looked like a little old lady you'd see in *Good Housekeeping* magazine, all the way down to her plain housedress and shoes. *What the Hell did she do?* She read on about how she had killed her husband and was suspected of killing all five of her former husbands. The article reported that the convicted woman was sure they would pardon her, and even more sure that at the very least, they would never hang her. Even up to the time they walked her to the gallows, she told the deputy, "I'm sure word from the governor will arrive any minute." But the article ended with the hanging shortly thereafter, and more gruesome than that, Eva Dugan's head popped off and rolled into the crowd. *Oh my God. How barbaric.*

She then read the name 'Dillinger.' She stepped closer and put her hand over her mouth, thinking, *John Dillinger, I'll be damned.* She read the account of how the Pima County Sheriff's captured his whole gang, and although Dillinger himself escaped, he was shot dead less than a year later.

Just then she heard Benny call her voice, "Mary!"

She looked up, wide-eyed, still in shock at some of the things the Pima County Sheriff's Department had accomplished. Mary suddenly understood this was no backward sheriff's department, and it scared her. "Hi… hi Benny."

Benny came over and picked up the box off the chair. He noticed she had been reading. "There's a lot of history on this wall, did you see the old lady they hung."

Mary felt scared and let out a deep exhale. "I saw it… I gotta go now, Benny."

Benny waved goodbye and glanced at the plaques. He still felt the same about the sheriff and deputies, and he knew he would never be hunted down by these yahoos.

21 *Eva Dugan*

York Times.

LATE CITY EDITION

TUESDAY, MAY 15, 1934. TWO CENTS

ROBLES GIRL AND GETTLE SAFE HOME; CHILD CHAINED IN PIT UNDER CACTUS; SIX SEIZED AS GETTLE'S KIDNAPPERS

GETTLE RESCUE SUDDEN

Raid on City Apartment Obtains a Clue to the Abductors' Lair.

VICTIM IS FOUND BOUND

One Thug Escapes From the House, but Is Rounded Up Later With Others.

NONE OF RANSOM IS PAID

W. F. GETTLE

JUNE ROBLES

CHILD 19 DAYS IN HOLE

Letter From Chicago Led Searchers to Desert, 10 Miles From Tucson.

EXHAUSTED, WILL RECOVER

Child Herself Unlocks Padlock of Chains With Key Found Near Grave-Like Pit.

2 ARRESTS BELIEVED NEAR

Cheering Crowds Welcome June as She Appears on Balcony of Her Home.

BROKER AIDE SEIZED

UNCLE TELLS STORY

22 *Robles Girl*

The Arizona Daily Star

DILLINGER GANG CAPTURED HERE

JOHNSON DENIES OPPRESSION OF SMALL BUSINESS

Delegation of Powers By Congress Monetary Issue

FULL STRENGTH NAVY PROMISED IN SEVEN YEARS

The National WHIRLIGIG

POLICE FORCED TO USE GUNS IN NABBING TWO GANGSTERS OTHERS SUBMIT TO OFFICERS

Three Dillinger Aides Arrested in Tucson

'Triggerman' Pulls Gun On Chief In City Lockup

IDENTITY IS SURE

Men Are Wanted In East For Murders, Bank Robberies

FOUR ARRESTED AFTER LYNCHING

Indiana Police Ask Return Of Three Dillinger Bandits

23 *Dillinger Captured*

CHAPTER 23

It was a hot spring night, almost nine months since Mary moved into the little cottage in the back of Benny and Irene's home. Benny laid awake in bed, waiting to make sure Irene was asleep. When he was sure, he quietly got up and took his late-night stroll back to the cottage. He did so regularly now, three to four times a week, usually just after 1 a.m. in the morning. Mary was always waiting, as she was this night. She let him into the dark cottage, helped him take his clothes off, and pulled him into her bed.

When they were finished, Benny sat up in bed and lit a cigarette, "Mary, I've made a decision."

"About what?" she asked.

"About us. I want to start our life together in Nevada."

"Nevada?" asked Mary.

"Yeah, in Las Vegas."

"Mary switched on the small lamp next to her bed. She propped herself up on her elbow. "Really, when?"

"I want to do it soon, real soon. But I want Stephen to come with us."

"Stephen needs to be here, with his momma. Hell, he doesn't even like me. I see it in his eyes, the way he stares at me, with such coldness in his heart. It's worse than hate I tell you."

"I don't care about that. I gotta get Stephen away from his momma. Irene is trying to ruin him. He's got talent like I do, and I'll be damned if I'm just gonna walk away. Now, are you coming with us?"

Mary was taken back by his sudden outburst. She laid back down and stared at the ceiling. She didn't like it one bit, but she loved Benny more than anything. "Let me think about it."

"Well think fast, because we have one more job before we leave."

She got back up on her elbow. "What the hell do you mean? We have plenty of money."

Benny was growing impatient now. "Not if Stephen's coming. I want a cushion. Besides, I must leave money for Irene. I must leave $6,000 of my money, plus give her the $4,500 that belongs to her. That'll give her $10,000 to take care of herself and the other three boys."

"Benny, we only have $16,000 left! How you gonna give her $6,000 when that's all we have to live on?"

"Mary aren't you listening, that's why we gotta rob one more bank. Then we'll be set."

"I don't like it." Mary had long ago decided she was not robbing banks anymore. After reading those historical plaques at the sheriff's office, she came to understand just how lucky they were to have gotten away, twice. She wasn't going to underestimate the sheriffs or deputies of the west, not after seeing their history on the wall. She imagined herself on that wall, captured, hung by the neck, or gunned down. Whatever it would be, she pictured herself on that wall, with Benny right beside her, and that was enough to stop her from ever going again.

Neither said a word. Mary broke the silence, "Listen, I'm telling you, I'll get by with less money. That's no problem. But Stephen will not be happy with us. He is not like us. Look what he did to those cats!"

"How the hell did you know about that?"

"I saw them, I saw what he did! He's not normal Benny! He needs to be raised by his momma."

"Bullshit! He needs me, I have to protect him! I understand that little shit."

"You're wrong Benny. He needs help. Besides, I told you he hates me." Mary was getting up the nerve to draw her own line in the sand very soon. She was not going to let Stephen come with them.

Benny said abruptly, "End of the conversation, he's coming with us."

Mary knew it was no use. But she had already made up her mind on another matter. "Well, I can't go on the bank job this time. I'm too afraid."

"No matter. I can go myself, I can steal the getaway car just as easily."

Mary was surprised to hear this after all his talk about how much he needed her. She said, "Well… if you've made up your mind, when are you going, and where?"

"I'm going to hit the same bank we did last time. Our FBI genius who they consult with said bank robbers rarely hit the same bank twice, especially when there are so many new branches popping up all over."

"When?" She started to fidget with her cigarette pack.

"I'm goin' Friday, in two days."

"When are we leaving for Vegas?" she asked.

"When I get back. We'll sell the store, and I'll start making arrangements, including letting Irene know that if she wants her damn money, Stephen's coming with me."

Benny got up and left. Mary said nothing but was boiling inside. After he was gone, she lit a cigarette and walked out to the cottage porch, sitting on a chair outside the front door. She was plotting in her mind how to take a stand, how to tell him it was her or Stephen. But she was scared. She tried to reason out in her mind if he'd leave her stranded for the sake of his son. *Hell, he's robbing a bank for that little shit, even though we have enough money to get out of here right now.* She suddenly felt doubtful about everything.

24 National Bank in Phoenix

CHAPTER 24

Two days later Benny pulled out of his driveway and headed to Phoenix. Everything started off as planned, but when Benny was switching back to his family Pontiac, a deputy patrol car saw him and recognized the getaway vehicle. Benny took off, and the deputy swung around, making a U-turn on a busy highway. Suddenly, another car slammed into the deputy's car. Benny heard the crash and looked in his mirror, quickly realizing he'd been given a lucky break. He took off north, heading away from Phoenix and zigzagged his way further west.

Benny knew the Pontiac had been seen, and there was a good chance they would looking for him. The deputy may have seen his license plate, but even if he hadn't, they might find him from the color and model of the car. He decided he had to drive through to Las Vegas to let things cool off.

Benny drove for a while, and as soon as he got to the outskirts of the next town, he found a phone and called home. The operator told him how much to deposit. He reached into his pants, suddenly realizing he had no change. He hung up and redialed the operator.

"Operator, may I help you?"

"I need to make a collect call." He gave the operator his home number. Irene answered and accepted the charges.

Benny spoke quickly. "Irene, it's Benny."

"Benny, why are you calling?"

"Listen to me carefully. Go get Mary right now."

"Why the hell would . . ."

He cut her off. "Goddammit! Do as you're told and go get her now!"

Irene slammed the phone down onto the table.

A few minutes later Mary came into the kitchen and took the phone from Irene. "Benny? What is it?"

"I think they made me Mary. Now listen, you need to get the money out of the cottage. Take all of it, wrap it up good, and bury it in the back foothills. Walk up for at least a half mile and mark the spot well."

"Ok, I'll do it," said Mary.

"You gotta do this now, they'll be coming to look for me once word gets down there."

"What am I gonna tell them?

"Just tell them assholes you work for me, that's all. Keep going to work, keep opening the shop. I'll get in touch with you. Mary, don't try to run, they will try to connect you. But don't worry, I'll make sure they know you never had anything to do with any of this. You just sit tight for a long time. Now go now. Oh, wait! One more thing, if anything happens to me, you give Irene the blue bag with her $4,500 in it. I want you to also give her the $6,000 I told you about too. Hide it for now, but when things cool down, give it to her. It's hers, you understand?"

Mary knew there was no way in hell she was giving Irene the

$6,000 if something happened to him. It would only endanger her, and besides, Irene would never take it. "All right Benny, I will."

Mary hung up and ran out the back door.

Irene hung up the phone in the other room. She had heard the whole conversation. She watched from the window as Mary went into the shed and grabbed a spade. Mary then leaned it against the cottage door and went inside. A few minutes later she came out carrying four small satchels. She picked up the spade, and headed out behind the cottage, in the direction of the foothills.

Irene had seen enough, she ran and got the rifle and went out after her. When she rounded the cottage, Mary was in plain sight heading up toward the desert foothills. Irene shouted, "Hold it, Mary."

Mary stopped and turned wide-eyed to see Irene walking toward her, holding a rifle with it pointed right at her. Mary could tell from the way she held it that she knew how to use it. Mary's heart dropped. She was caught. She felt like running, like crying, but she stood there as Irene moved closer. The pictures on the wall of the sheriff's office suddenly flashed into her mind.

"Look here," said Irene, "I know you had nothing to do with where Benny got that money, I heard him say so. But as sure as my name is Irene Paddock, $4,500 of it belongs to me. It's from my daddy, and I brought it here with us. Now you're gonna give me that blue bag of money right now. I don't care about anything else Benny has done, that's all on him. But I'm not being stuck out here in Arizona with four boys and no money to raise my family."

Mary could not believe her ears. "He wanted you to have more."

"I don't want any more. Just give me my money."

Mary had thought Irene was going to take all the money, or worse, attempt citizen's arrest. She felt overwhelmingly relieved, and she calmly said, so as not to upset where things stood: "That's fine with me Irene, but we have to talk about one little thing."

"Talk," said Irene.

Mary swallowed, and said, "You and I don't know each other very well. That is the truth. But those deputies don't need to know anything else. Just tell them, I work in Benny's shop, and I pay rent. Tell them I am not very sociable. I'll tell them the same, that we do nothing more than saying 'hi' and 'goodbye,' that's the way it really is, so you won't be lying."

"That's fine with me," said Irene, keeping the gun pointed at her. "It's the truth as far I know anyway." Irene wasn't going to tell her she knew Benny had been laying with her for the last year.

"Then here," said Mary. She threw the blue bag of money over toward Irene. Irene picked it up and slowly backed away, keeping the gun pointed till she was at a safe distance, then headed to the shed to grab another spade. She went to their garden behind the house, dug a two-foot-deep hole, wrapped the satchel in plastic and buried it. Irene then moved some plants around, putting a few on top, and then smoothed out the dirt. She went inside, took off her dirty clothes and put them in the washer. Then went into the kitchen to look out the back window.

As she stood there, thinking about what had just happened, she exhaled deeply, calming herself. For the first time in what seemed like forever, she felt hope. She felt like everything was going to turn out. She had found the courage to use the rifle, and had gotten her money. She thought for a moment, *those rifle lessons sure paid off.* She smiled, staring out the kitchen window, knowing she would soon be rid of both Benny and Mary, and that suited her just fine.

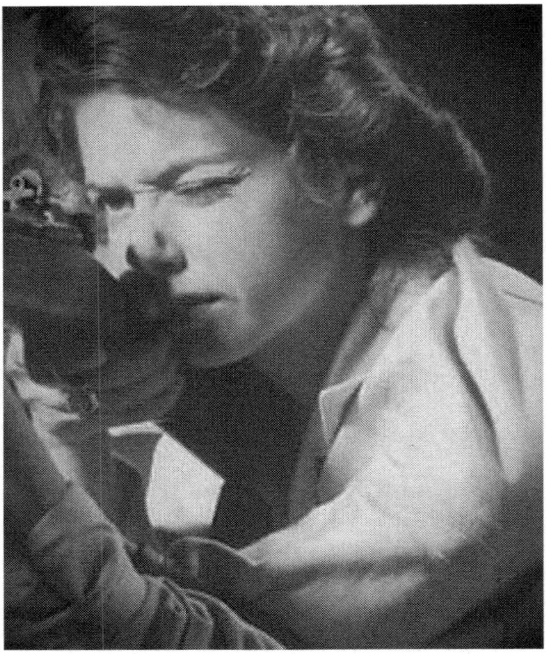

25 Irene Gets Her Money Back

CHAPTER 25

Benny drove into the night toward Las Vegas. Early the next morning he spotted a factory not far from the highway and waited for the parking lot to quiet down and the shift to start. Then he ditched his car in the woods a mile away and walked back to the plant parking lot and hotwired a car.

He drove into the bustling city of Las Vegas a little after eight in the morning and began making plans to set up a new identity. He didn't know, but someone at the plant witnessed the heist of the car, and it was already reported stolen to the Las Vegas police. The FBI was also alerted, as they had figured out Benny's identity and predicted he'd be driving a stolen car.

He was at the counter of a gas station purchasing gas when he saw them. Two federal agents pulled up and parked on the other side of the lot. "Shit!" he said aloud to the surprised clerk.

In the mid-morning heat of Las Vegas, Benny pulled his snub-nosed pistol from the back of his pants and charged out. Immediately the FBI car raced toward him. Benny pulled the trigger, shooting at their front windshield. The FBI car then screeched to a halt, and both doors flew open. Benny ran over and jumped in his car, wheeling around the lot. One of the agents ran toward him, pointing his gun, firing shots. Benny ducked and veered his car right at the agent, grazing him, knocking him down, as he slammed into a barrier, hitting his head. Benny shook it off and jumped out with blood running down his forehead. He pulled out his gun, and turned ready to engage them, when a voice from behind him shouted, "Freeze!"

Benny slowly dropped his gun and raised his arms. "Dammit!" he yelled, as they knocked him to the ground.

After he was captured, the news was relayed to the Pima County Sheriff's office. Within an hour Sheriff Burr and two deputies showed up at Irene's home. They searched the entire house and grounds but found nothing. They questioned both women extensively, but because the robberies were all committed alone, they quickly settled on the conclusion that Benny acted alone. In truth, Irene did not know that Mary was involved, and they never asked her about any hidden money.

Three weeks later Irene saw Mary getting into her car. She walked out to catch her in the driveway.

Mary stopped the car and rolled down the window. "What is it?"

"We need to talk," said Irene, stepping one step closer to the window.

"About what?" asked Mary in an annoyed tone.

Irene said plainly, "I think you should be moving on soon."

"No, not yet," said Mary, shaking her head slightly. "I know you don't like me, but I think it's best everything stays the same for a good while. It will raise less suspicion."

Irene was quiet for a moment. "That's fine with me, for a while.

But I want you to know, I told the boys Benjamin was killed in a car accident. I'm transferring them to a new school this fall. I need you to honor all that."

"I don't talk to your boys."

"Fine, I don't care what happens to Benjamin, and I don't want to know. We are through with him, and he's never coming back here."

Mary shifted back in her seat and smirked, "That's fine with me."

"You need to be thinking about getting a move on as soon as you can, weeks, maybe a month, maybe two, but no more."

Mary looked at her and said sternly, "I understand what you want. Once I feel things have blown over, I will leave, not before."

Irene turned and went back into the house.

26 *Sheriff Burr*

Mazzuca Awaits Sanity Hearing

Weather

49'er

Las Vegas REVIEW-JOURNAL

NEVADA'S LARGEST AND MOST COMPLETE NEWSPAPER

VEGAS G-MEN FIRE ON ROBBERY SUSPECT

GOP MASTERMINDS

Nixon Selects Top Planners

Wanted Man Captured Here

SANITY

Mazzuca Awaits Hearing

GRANT RESIGNS

James Gibson Jury Foreman

VEGAS MILESTONE

50,000th Telephone For Southern Nevada

Fighting Campaign, Says Lodge

Congratulations From Kennedy Go to Nixon

Sandwich Title Goes To Nevadan

Nixon Shares GOP Attention With Goldwater

NEWS

Officials Discuss Need For Hospital Expansion

STORY OF CAPTURE

Mazzuca Capers

ON THE INSIDE

27 Benny Caught by G – Men

28 *Benny In the News*

CHAPTER 26

Three months after Benny was caught, Stephen, still 11, was lying in his room thinking about the concert so long ago. He imagined himself pulling out his knife and slicing the throats of those two boys who hurt him, thinking, *they did this to my daddy. They embarrassed him, they beat him, they are Mary's kind*. Now his mind zeroed in on Mary. She was his real enemy, having stolen his dad from the family by her wily ways. He waved the imaginary knife through the air, slicing Mary's throat, then stabbing her in the stomach to be sure.

He drifted off to sleep and dreamt he saw the dark-hooded figure smiling at him with steely grey eyes and dark stringy hair. It said nothing but only stared at him. Stephen woke up and heard the whisper. *Kill Mary, Kill Mary.*

Stephen sat up thinking for a moment. It was a dark moonless night, and everyone was asleep. He then got out of bed, threw on his shoes and crept into the living room, making his way to the kitchen. He slowly opened the knife drawer and took out a large knife. He went out the back door and walked along the path leading to the cottage.

Although he was scared, there was also a feeling of dark, sweet confidence coming over him. He saw a light on in the back room of the cottage. He went to the side window and peered in to see Mary laying on her bed watching the television, wearing only a short sheer nightgown. Stephen could see her body clearly through the flimsy material. He watched her for a while, it was the first time he had seen a woman nearly naked.

He went around the front of the cottage and slowly turned the knob and gently pushed the door, but it was bolted. He grimaced, then went around to the other side of the cottage, carefully scanning the windows. The kitchen window was ajar. He carefully lifted it, as slowly as he could, making no noise, and crawled inside. The rage began to build. From the kitchen, he could see a ray of light from the bedroom light shining into the living room. He walked into it, toward the bedroom knowing Mary would be right inside the door, facing away from him. He crept forward, silent step by silent step. He peered in, taking in her legs stretched out on the bed. He knew he had to strike quickly, but he was afraid, so he waited, but the rage grew stronger. Finally, he collected himself and stepped into the room, brandishing the large knife.

"What the hell are you doing?" Mary screamed as she instinctively rolled off the other side of the bed. Stephen had been too slow. He now circled around the bed, wide-eyed, fixed on his plan, all the while keeping his eyes directly on her. Mary bent down and pulled a pistol from under her pillow and pointed it right at his face. "Drop the knife, right now, drop it." She cocked the hammer.

Stephen froze for a moment as if shaken out of a bad dream, and dropped the knife.

Mary walked over to him and pointed the gun right at his forehead. "I'll blow your head off if you move." She carefully watched his response. She could see he was scared out of his wits.

"What are you doing here! Oh, I see. Are you coming back here to get what your daddy's been getting, Stephen? Are you?"

Stephen shook his head.

Mary knew she had to frighten him good, or else she might not be so lucky next time. She knew she needed to drive the fear of God into him. "Let's see what a man you are. Pull your pants down!"

Stephen's eyes widened in fear, but he was too afraid to move. He felt the rage rising,

Mary raised the pistol higher, holding it firmly at arm's length and cocked the lever back, saying with gritted teeth, "I said, pull them down now!"

Stephen closed his eyes and pulled his pants down. Mary laughed, "Look at you. You are a little sissy, just like your daddy always said you were, you'll never be like him!"

Mary took a step closer, while putting the gun under his chin, forcing him to his toes. She pressed her nearly naked body up against the side of his thigh. "What's wrong, Stephen?" she said in a condescending soft voice.

Stephen shuddered, he was scared out of his mind. Mary looked down and saw a small puddle on the floor. She backed away, knowing she had pushed far enough. "I should blow your head right off right this minute."

Tears started rolling down Stephen's cheek.

Mary yelled, "Turn around!"

Stephen turned, and Mary stepped back slightly, keeping the gun pointed at his head. "If you ever come near this place again, I'll blow your head off. Do you understand?"

Stephen nodded; he needed to get out.

Mary snapped, "Now get the hell out of here."

Stephen pulled up his pants and ran out the front door, across the yard, and slipped quietly back into the house. He went to his room and laid in bed shaking, raging, screaming in his mind. He cried himself to sleep and the next day woke up to find his bed soaking-wet.

The next day Irene came out to drive Stephen and his brothers to school. Mary was outside her cottage in a chair watching. Stephen looked over, and they stared at each other for a moment. Mary knew he was regathering his courage. She watched Irene get them all into the car, but she mainly watched Stephen.

Once inside the car, he looked over again, and as soon as his mom pulled away, he gave her the finger.

Mary felt scared seeing his icy stare. She knew he could have killed her. She said aloud to herself, "That kid is a psycho."

As soon they were out of sight, Mary went up into the hills and retrieved the money she had hidden. She gathered whatever she could and got in Benny's Cadillac. She took one last look at the place, "Forget this place, I'm outta here."

29 *Mary Jaycox Says Goodbye*

CHAPTER 27

The incident in Mary's cottage had thrust Stephen's psyche into a dark frightful storm. He began wetting the bed weekly, and the rage now came back to him more and more.

The following summer the family pulled up stakes in Tucson and moved to Sacramento California. They rented a small house in a poor neighborhood by the freeway. Irene had time to get a job now since all the four boys were in school. She still had a good amount of the money left, which she vowed to invest for the boys.

Stephen began high school that fall, but his turmoil did not subside. He was a loner from the start. He was tall, skinny, and looked frail in the face. He wasn't particularly attractive, but it didn't matter because he was scared of girls and wanted nothing to do with them. He really wanted nothing to do with anybody.

He was often bullied before and after school, but he did not care. All it did was cement in his mind who his enemies were. He knew someday he would get back at them, just like he would get back at Mary Jaycox.

Stephen was no star athlete, but he noticed he was fast and limber. In freshman gym class, they spent two weeks playing tennis and Stephen was hooked. He began playing after school, hitting balls against a building wall not from their house. The following spring, he tried out for the tennis team and made the practice squad, the next year, he made the real team.

Stephen excelled in his grades, especially in math. By his senior year, he was starting to feel a small degree of self-esteem. He still wet the bed occasionally, but only his mom knew, and it was getting better. Near the end of his senior year, Stephen was in the locker room showering with the other boys on the team. He was lost in thought, and had just finished washing his privates, and was now rinsing himself when he heard someone laugh.

One of the boys in the shower shouted, "Getting excited, Paddock." Then the boys started to laugh.

Stephen snapped out of his daze and looked down at himself, he had a hard-on. He quickly ran out of the shower and dressed, not even bothering to dry off. He left to their howls and laughter, running home from school, stressed and humiliated beyond imagination. He went straight to his room, lying on his bed, feeling his anger build.

The next day he reluctantly went to school, but as soon as he arrived, he felt a hundred sets of eyes on him. He heard their whispers even though they were only in his head. In his paranoid mind, they all knew what happened to him in the shower. He decided to skip school and went home, telling his mom he was sick after she came home from work.

All that night Stephen laid in bed thinking about how much he needed his father. He also thought of Mary, the woman who ruined his life. He began making a mental list of all the people he was to make pay someday, and he put Mary Jaycox at the top.

He refused to go back to school, but it didn't matter, Stephen was an excellent student and was able to make up his tests. He skipped graduation and said goodbye to high school.

30 Stephen School Picture

31 Stephen Tennis Team

CHAPTER 28

After driving away from the cottage and from her life in Tucson, Mary began a new life under an assumed name, taking a job as a clerk in Las Vegas. She enjoyed the nightlife in the city and had plenty of money from which to draw on, though she used it sparingly.

She found various lovers to replace Benny, but no one excited her as he did. They were all meager substitutes, none of which she let stay around long enough to become attached. Over time she ran down Benny's case and discovered that he had been sentenced to 20 years in a Federal penitentiary.

She missed him terribly; there was nothing she could do to get him out of her mind. In the summer of 1965, after four years of missing him, she decided it was safe enough to pay him a visit. She dyed her hair blonde and rented a room north of El Paso, some 30 miles from the prison. She fictitiously changed her name to Mary Paddock and had a fake New Mexico driver's license made. Finally, after spending several months trying to work up her courage, she went to see Benny. She told the guards she was his sister from Wisconsin.

For the next two years, she visited Benny once a week. She found a little waitress job down in El Paso to keep her busy, and to bring in some money. Occasionally she went out to a local nightspot, bringing home one-night stands to feed her sexual urges.

In 1967, after a year and a half of visits, she and Benny hatched their plan. Step one was for Mary to get in with one of the guards. To accomplish this, several times a day, Mary would drive up past the La Tuna Federal Penitentiary to Anthony, Texas, and then back down. She watched the guards leave work, getting to know which ones headed toward El Paso, writing down what kind of cars they drove. Once she had her list, she began her next phase of the plan.

Mary started driving past all the bars in the nearby small towns between Anthony and El Paso. Her first hit happened after three days. She fixed herself up and went into the bar. There at the bar, talking to some men, was one of the guards. Mary smiled, walked up near them and ordered a beer.

She saw the men looking at her, and she acted bashfully. Then she noticed the guard carefully slip off his wedding ring and put it in his pocket. Mary took a sip, laid down some money and left. Her plan wouldn't work with a married man.

Two days later she spotted another one of the cars at a diner halfway between the prison and El Paso. Mary went in and saw the good-looking man in plain clothes. She walked up, carefully eyeing his ring finger; there was no ring. She smiled at him, "Excuse me, can you help me? I just moved here recently. I need to buy a good set of small tools for fixing little things around my apartment."

The man smiled at her, intrigued, "Well what are you trying to fix?"

"Oh, there's always something, like hanging pictures and things like that."

"There's a hardware store down the highway a few exits, they could put something together for you."

"Thank you, this is my first time here, what do you

recommend?"

"Are you by yourself?"

She smiled, "Yes, I am, I'm afraid."

"Well if you care to join me, you'd be most welcome."

"Why that's nice of you." Mary smiled and sat down.

"My name is Jimmy, Jimmy Fields."

"Hello Jimmy Fields, I'm Mary Paddock."

They immediately clicked, as Mary hoped they would. By the end of the meal, he asked for her number. Mary politely made an excuse. But she made sure she kept going to that diner running into him and frequently sitting down to eat with him, or to have a cup of coffee. He asked her more than a few times if she would go out with him, but Mary kept telling him she wasn't ready. She said, she couldn't say why, but someday she would tell him. But they would sit, and eat, and talk… always enjoying each other's company.

One night, after dinner, she asked him to take a walk with her. She pretended to cry and let out her secret. "Jimmy I'm sorry, I don't want to lead you on. The reason I'm here is because of my brother. I came up here to try to build a life nearby so I could visit him in prison. I got no one special back home, just my mom, and dad. My dad is sick, but they still take care of each other."

"Who is your brother?"

"Benjamin Paddock, he goes by Benny, but we call him Junior."

"Benny? Oh, I know who he is. I heard he's a nice guy, kind of a big fella, and funny."

"That's Junior. He's always watched out for me and made me laugh. I know he's done some things, but he's my brother, and I love him. Now you know the reason I can't date you. You can't be dating an inmate's sister."

"Why not? I'm not gonna' tell anybody."

Mary was quiet for a moment. "Aren't there people around here who know you work at the prison?"

"Yeah, but not really, I keep to myself except for stopping here. Besides, I live down in El Paso; it's a great big town down there with lots of people. No one is gonna know you got someone in the prison unless you tell them."

Mary heard exactly what she needed to hear. She looked at the ground, "I've told no one. I'm ashamed."

"Well then it will be our secret, now will you go out with me?"

Mary smiled, and batted her eyelashes, "I sure would like that."

Jimmy smiled widely, and leaned over, kissing her on the cheek.

That innocent kiss began a long slow fuse relationship. Mary pretended to be an innocent, one who would never jump into bed with just anyone before she was engaged. After a few months of going out on dates, Jimmy surprised her and proposed.

Mary enthusiastically accepted and asked him if they could wait a year, to give them time to get to know each other. Jimmy had no reservations with that, and they set the day for exactly one year away. Coming home that night, they fell into bed, and their whirlwind romance started.

Jimmy was head over heels in love with Mary, and she was good at pretending to be. Within a few months, she moved into his apartment in El Paso.

Mary played the loving, doted on fiancé very well, but inwardly she was waiting for a sign that would tell her it was time for the next phase of the plan.

32 *Diner Near El Paso*

33 *La Tuna Federal Penitentiary*

CHAPTER 29

In early November that year Mary wrote herself a note and signed it with her fake mother's name, Stella Paddock. She folded it several times and crinkled it just a little, then waited for Jimmy to come home. When he walked into the apartment after work, he found her crying at the kitchen table with the note in her hand.

"What's wrong?"

"Everything's wrong," said Mary, wiping her eyes with a tissue.

Suddenly worried he could lose her, Jimmy asked, "What do you mean everything's wrong?"

Mary shook her head, "Oh, I should have told you sooner Jimmy, I'm pregnant."

A sigh of relief went through him. "Well that's great news, we'll get married now." He went over to her and knelt, putting his hand on her knee.

"I want that too Jimmy, I'm 39 years old, and I've always dreamed of having a family." She began to cry harder. "But now… now I don't know what I'm going to do." Mary was hoping she sounded convincing.

"What do you mean, Mary? I'll take care of you." Jimmy loved her deeply, and he too wanted a family. He was also in his late 30s and had never found the right woman until he met Mary.

"You don't understand, I can't stay here any longer, not now." Mary turned away, whisking the letter with her.

"Why not? What's wrong?" He asked, now more puzzled than ever.

"Because of this!" She dramatically whisked the letter back and handed it to him. Jimmy took it, still puzzled, and began to read.

My Dearest Mary,

I'm sorry to tell you this, but your father has died. We buried him last week at the old cemetery outside the church. He was calling for you, he wanted to see you, but I did not know how to reach you in time. His last words were about our dear Junior. Your daddy said that he still believed Junior was innocent, and that he wished he were still home to take care of me.

Mary, I need your help. With your daddy gone now and Junior unjustly imprisoned, there is no one to help me. I'm running out of resources, and I have very little money. I fear I will be the next to go if you don't get home soon. Please tell Junior that I love him, and I miss him terribly.

Mom

Jimmy looked up with emotions racing, piecing together a plan. "I'm sorry about your dad, Mary. Listen, I'll go home with you. I'll marry you, and we can move home and take care of your mom."

"No!" She sobbed.

"What do you mean?"

Mary cried harder and shook her head, "You don't understand,

I could never do that to her. You're a lawman. Hell, you're one of Junior's jailers. Someone will find out, and it will destroy her." Mary looked down, fidgeting with her fingers, "No, you stay here where your life is. I'll go home for now, after momma dies, I'll come back." She shook her head in disappointment, and feebly added, "Maybe we can travel sometimes, or maybe you can come to see me, kind of in secret."

She dropped the letter on the floor, and walked off into her room, making sure to burst into tears as soon as she closed the door.

Jimmy sat thinking. He was sure of his love for her, and this was his one chance at having a family, his chance at real love, the love he always wanted but could never find. He went to the bedroom and knocked, "Mary, I'm coming in." He opened the door and saw her lying across the bed face down with her hands in her face, crying. "Mary, what if there was a way?"

"A way for what?" she said sorrowfully between sobs.

He sat on the edge of the bed and said, "A way… for Junior to go home."

"What are you talking about?"

"Mary, you said no one knows anything about Junior's parents, or where he's from. Is that true?"

"Yes," she said, keeping her face in her hands.

"Are you certain?"

"Of course, I am." Mary knew it was the moment of truth.

"Well, what if I could get Junior out. What if Junior could go home to help your momma? Would he?"

Mary rolled over, looking up at him with tear stained eyes, "What are you talking about?"

"I think I can get him outside the prison. But getting away will be up to him."

Mary now sat up, "Jimmy, don't be giving me false hope about something' so important to me."

"I'm not, I know this is important to you."

"Oh, Jimmy." Mary thrust her arms around him. "I don't want to leave you. I want to have our family together and grow old with you right here in Texas."

Jimmy helped her to stand and helped her into the living room. "In three weeks we're having a New Year's Eve party for all the staff of the prison. We're gonna have at least 20 orderlies, picked from the prisoners, who are going to work in the kitchen and help serve. I'll make sure Benny is chosen. I'll also make sure he can help the cooks with any preparation. He's must cut his arm very severely, I'm afraid. I've seen it done, a few years ago a prisoner got cut bad. We had to take him to the hospital, and since it was on Christmas day, there was a light staff. I remember we cuffed the prisoner's hands and feet to the hospital bed. He was there all night alone.

"Jimmy, you think this will work?"

"There's just one risk. I can get you the key for the cuffs. But you're going to' have to get the key to him. I figure we can get a used car for the getaway and put it a few blocks from the hospital. You can drive down there in my car and be waiting, and after say, maybe 1 in the morning, go in, and give him the keys, then drive home. I'll have one of the boys bring me home, I'll make an excuse I've had a few drinks. You just gotta tell Benny to head west first. Then north up through Oregon and he can travel across the top of the country. They won't be searching' up there, so far away."

"Oh my God Jimmy. Will it work?"

"I think it will. Like I said, the only risk is you giving him the key. But it's really no risk at all. If someone stops you, just tell them you're coming to see your brother. Keep the key in your bra so there'll be no trouble. You just open one shackle, give him the keys and quietly come home. The rest, getting the other three shackles off and getting outside, will be up to him. Is that clear? That keeps you safe."

"I'll do it!" Mary said bravely.

"Well, then you go and talk to Benny tomorrow during visiting hours. The cuts gotta be real deep. Lots of blood and needing lots of stitches. Right here is the best place." Jimmy drew a line across his lower forearm. Benny should be screaming and bleeding everywhere. I'll give you the rest of the details, including the time it should happen. What do you think Mary?" He exhaled deeply, wondering if he'd covered everything.

"I think only one thing. I love you, and I will never forget this."

Mary made all the arrangements. She spoke with Benny, and everything was set. On New Year's Eve, at the appointed time, Benny cut deep. They called an ambulance, and a prison guard rode with him to the hospital with a deputy car behind them. Benny had lost so much blood they hooked him up to an IV and temporarily stitched the large wound. They handcuffed his legs and one arm to the bed and left, leaving instructions that they would collect him in the morning at first light.

Mary sat outside in the getaway car. She had already ditched Jimmy's car. She watched the deputy car pull away and waited another half hour until just after midnight. She went in and took the stairs up and walked down the quiet hall into his room. She unhooked the IV, undid the shackles on his hands and feet, and helped him into the clothes she had brought. She handed him a loaded pistol and gave him a warm kiss. She looked outside the room and waved him down the hall to the stairs to their waiting getaway car.

Two hours later, at 2:30 a.m. Jimmy Fields was dropped off by his friend. He went inside his apartment and turned on the lights. There was a note, and something wrapped in paper sitting on the table. He called out, "Mary?" There was no answer. His heart started to race as he picked up the note.

My dear Jimmy,

I know you may never understand because, in some ways, I did love you. I just love Benny more. Know, that I will always remember your bravery in setting forth this plan. But as you may gather, I had to change things up some.

I've enclosed a copy of the cassette tape I had recording when we set our plan in motion that night you knocked on the bedroom door. Don't worry. I'll never use it. You have a copy, I have a copy, and my good friend has a copy in case anything ever happens to me.

Don't worry either about any baby, I am not pregnant. Jimmy, I want to close by telling you, the days I spent with you were nice. I hope you don't get caught, because I'd hate to think what all them boys would do to you if you were in prison.

Mary

PS: Your car is parked where the getaway car was. The keys are under the passenger mat.

"Goddamn!" Jimmy shouted, as he fell backward onto his living couch, shaking his head, "I'll be goddammed!"

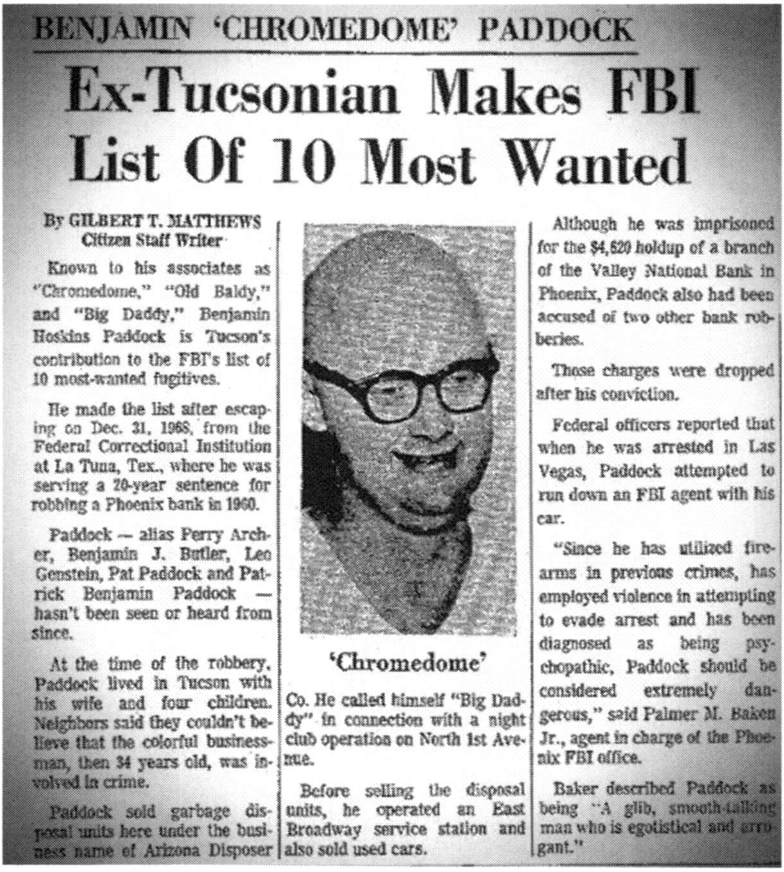

BENJAMIN 'CHROMEDOME' PADDOCK

Ex-Tucsonian Makes FBI List Of 10 Most Wanted

By GILBERT T. MATTHEWS
Citizen Staff Writer

Known to his associates as "Chromedome," "Old Baldy," and "Big Daddy," Benjamin Hoskins Paddock is Tucson's contribution to the FBI's list of 10 most-wanted fugitives.

He made the list after escaping on Dec. 31, 1968, from the Federal Correctional Institution at La Tuna, Tex., where he was serving a 20-year sentence for robbing a Phoenix bank in 1960.

Paddock — alias Perry Archer, Benjamin J. Butler, Leo Genstein, Pat Paddock and Patrick Benjamin Paddock — hasn't been seen or heard from since.

At the time of the robbery, Paddock lived in Tucson with his wife and four children. Neighbors said they couldn't believe that the colorful businessman, then 34 years old, was involved in crime.

Paddock sold garbage disposal units here under the business name of Arizona Disposer Co. He called himself "Big Daddy" in connection with a night club operation on North 1st Avenue.

Before selling the disposal units, he operated an East Broadway service station and also sold used cars.

'Chromedome'

Although he was imprisoned for the $4,620 holdup of a branch of the Valley National Bank in Phoenix, Paddock also had been accused of two other bank robberies.

Those charges were dropped after his conviction.

Federal officers reported that when he was arrested in Las Vegas, Paddock attempted to run down an FBI agent with his car.

"Since he has utilized firearms in previous crimes, has employed violence in attempting to evade arrest and has been diagnosed as being psychopathic, Paddock should be considered extremely dangerous," said Palmer M. Baker Jr., agent in charge of the Phoenix FBI office.

Baker described Paddock as being "A glib, smooth-talking man who is egotistical and arrogant."

[34] *Most Wanted*

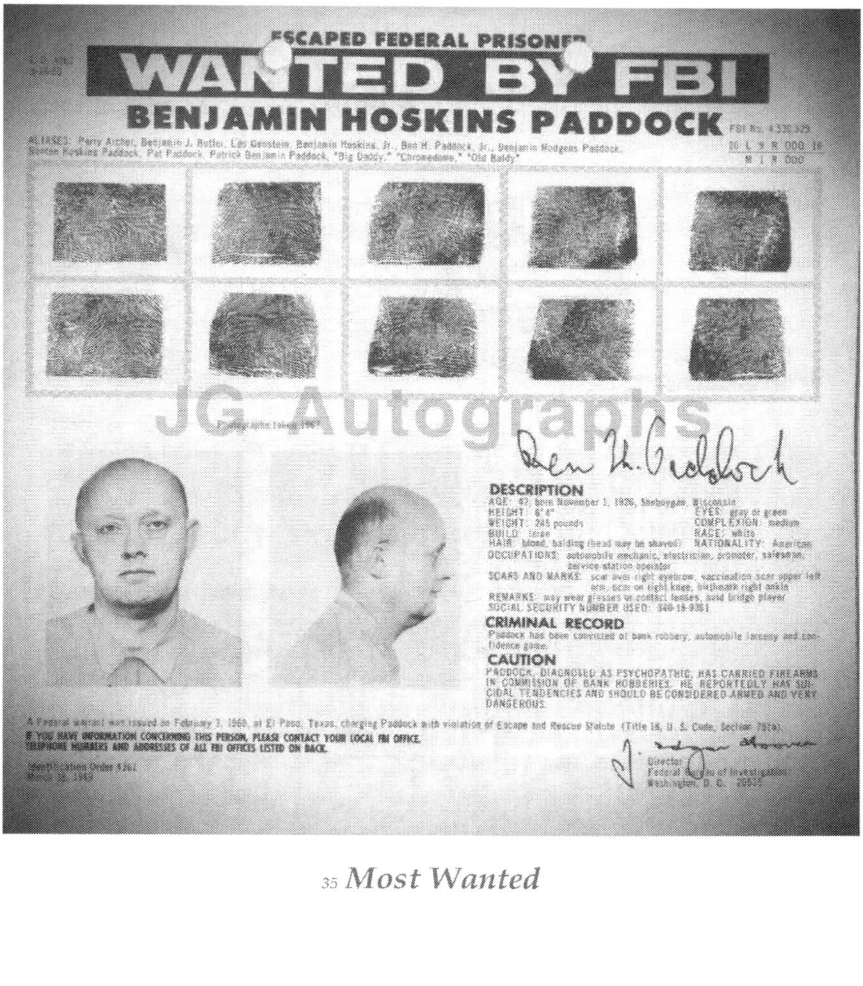

ESCAPED FEDERAL PRISONER

WANTED BY FBI

BENJAMIN HOSKINS PADDOCK

FBI No. 4,330,925

20 L 9 R 000 16
M 1 R 000

ALIASES: Perry Archer, Benjamin J. Butler, Leo Genstein, Benjamin Hoskins, Jr., Ben H. Paddock, Jr., Benjamin Hodgens Paddock, Benton Hoskins Paddock, Pat Paddock, Patrick Benjamin Paddock, "Big Daddy," "Chromedome," "Old Baldy"

Photographs taken 1967

DESCRIPTION

AGE: 42, born November 1, 1926, Sheboygan, Wisconsin
HEIGHT: 6'4" EYES: gray or green
WEIGHT: 245 pounds COMPLEXION: medium
BUILD: large RACE: white
HAIR: blond, balding (head may be shaved) NATIONALITY: American
OCCUPATIONS: automobile mechanic, electrician, promoter, salesman, service station operator
SCARS AND MARKS: scar over right eyebrow, vaccination scar upper left arm, scar on right knee, birthmark right ankle
REMARKS: may wear glasses or contact lenses, avid bridge player
SOCIAL SECURITY NUMBER USED: 340-16-9361

CRIMINAL RECORD

Paddock has been convicted of bank robbery, automobile larceny and confidence game.

CAUTION

PADDOCK, DIAGNOSED AS PSYCHOPATHIC, HAS CARRIED FIREARMS IN COMMISSION OF BANK ROBBERIES. HE REPORTEDLY HAS SUICIDAL TENDENCIES AND SHOULD BE CONSIDERED ARMED AND VERY DANGEROUS.

A Federal warrant was issued on February 3, 1969, at El Paso, Texas, charging Paddock with violation of Escape and Rescue Statute (Title 18, U. S. Code, Section 751a).

IF YOU HAVE INFORMATION CONCERNING THIS PERSON, PLEASE CONTACT YOUR LOCAL FBI OFFICE. TELEPHONE NUMBERS AND ADDRESSES OF ALL FBI OFFICES LISTED ON BACK.

Identification Order 4261
March 10, 1969

Director
Federal Bureau of Investigation
Washington, D. C. 20535

35 *Most Wanted*

CHAPTER 30

Stephen's Adult Years

Stephen was 19 and attending community college, living near campus by himself. He was a loner and plagued by frequent nightmares, nightmares of being hunted down by Mary, and of her putting the gun to his throat and pulling the trigger. He would wake shaking, and once he calmed down, think about the ways he could finish what he tried to do that night so long ago.

Stephen would frequently visit an adult bookstore near his home, which pulled him deeper into the warped sexuality that came from his tumultuous youth. On the outside, he appeared to be a quiet nerd who liked math and kept to himself, but inside he was deeply frustrated and raging against the world.

On a rare, cold wintry day in California, Stephen opened his mailbox in the hall of his apartment and rifled through the mail. He saw a handwritten envelope post-marked from Idaho with no return address. He thought, *Who the hell lives in Idaho?*

He immediately opened it and found himself unfolding an old newspaper clipping.

June 10, 1969, El Paso Post

A convict who escaped from La Tuna Federal Correctional Institute near El Paso last New Year's Eve has been placed on the FBI's Ten Most Wanted list. Benjamin Hoskins Paddock was serving a 20-year sentence for robbing a Phoenix bank in 1960. He was also under indictment on charges of robbing two other banks. When arrested in Las Vegas he attempted to run down an FBI agent and had to be stopped by gunfire. He has been known to be armed.

Known as "Chrome-dome," "Old Badly," and "Big Daddy," Paddock is 6 feet 4 inches tall and weighs 245 pounds. He is balding and often shaves his head completely. Anyone with information should contact the FBI or the nearest law enforcement agency.

Stephen's heart began to race, and his hands began to shake. He tried to curse, but stopped himself, knowing the neighbors might hear. *Who the Hell sent this to me?* He turned the envelope over, hoping to find the answer, but there was none. He then muttered through seething teeth, "It's that bitch Mary Jaycox."

He went to his apartment, furious and trembling, as the rage screamed aloud in his brain. He grabbed a bottle of brandy and chugged it for a moment, hoping to calm his nerves, and reread the article. He could not believe it; his dad was alive.

The boiling anger and confusion escalated over the next several weeks and months. So, did his dreams about Mary. He knew she was haunting him. He tried going to libraries, looking for information from Idaho in newspapers, but it was fruitless. There was nothing to be found. One night his rage was so great that he burst out of his bed screaming. He calmed himself down and sat on the couch drinking for almost a half hour, then went out into the night for a walk.

He ended up walking to an area in downtown Sacramento where there were lots of prostitutes as well as homeless people. It was here he heard the soothing dark voice again. *Stephen,*

Stephen. The voice told him nothing specific, but Stephen knew what it wanted. He kept walking for hours, feeling his rage toward Mary building, now feeling the pressure too, afraid his dad would come back and find out that he was a failure.

The next evening Stephen went to a hardware store and bought some things, just in case he needed them, and went to bed. A few hours later the voice woke him. Stephen laid awake, feeling the rage building stronger than it had been in years. He grabbed what he needed and went out this time in his car. He knew who he was looking for; he had seen her walking the night before.

It took over an hour, but he found her: a slim, older-looking prostitute with long black hair. She was walking along a downtown street wearing sheer pantyhose and a short skirt. Stephen pulled up and smiled through his rolled down window. "Hello."

She walked over, "How are you, young man?"

Stephen did not know what to say. "Umm, how much can I pay you?"

"$100 up front, for anything you want."

Stephen nodded, "Ok, that's good."

She got in, and Stephen handed her the money. He felt his anger growing as he drove to the secluded place he had found the night before. "Let's get in the back seat."

Stephen got out, clenching his left hand shut, and got into the back seat. He pulled his pants down. She got in the other side. "You want a blow job, hun?"

Stephen nodded. He knew he was not hard at all, but his mind was on fire with rage.

She smiled, knelt on the seat and lowered her head down, periodically working him with her hands, trying to get him started.

All Stephen could see was Mary. He opened his left hand and reached over her head with his right hand and grabbed wire he had bought earlier. He quickly thrust it around her neck and yanked as hard as he could, twisting, cutting off her feeble attempt to scream. She kicked wildly, grabbing his cock with her hand, trying to hurt him, but Stephen pulled harder and upwards, forcing her to let go and grab for her own throat. She kicked and thrashed in a violent attempt to break free. Tears were coming from her eyes and drops of blood from her neck. Soon, her thrashing began to slow, then suddenly it stopped, as her body fell limp in his hands.

Stephen held the wires firm, yanking even harder, though she was still. He closed his eyes, feeling his racing heart, feeling the rage slowly turn to sweet darkness. In his mind, he had just killed Mary.

He got out and grimaced. She had torn the skin on his cock with her nails, and he was bleeding. He closed the door and drove to a nearby woods. On the way, he saw it: a police car cruising slowly in the other direction. Stephen panicked, his heart began pounding harder than it ever had. She was laying on the floor of his backseat.

The patrol car passed, and after a few moments of glancing into his side mirrors, Stephen let out a loud exhale, and he felt the wetness in his pants, not from blood; he had pissed himself.

He drove for a while now, getting far from there, and went to the outskirts of the city. He found a place that looked safe, pulled over, and dragged the dead woman's body into the woods. He then drove toward home and stopped at a liquor store to buy a bottle of scotch. He went home and drank a third of the bottle, then laid awake for a long while worried that the police were going to find him. He vowed not to ever listen to that voice again.

Finally, he fell asleep, and for the first time in as long as he could remember, he slept soundly. The next day he calmly got up, showered, and left for class. Strangely, as he walked up to the campus, he felt peace he had not felt in years. He realized he had done the thing he needed to do, and it was over.

36 ***Prostitute***

CHAPTER 31

Several years later Stephen graduated with a degree in accounting. He got a job at a local manufacturer in the accounting department handling all the accounts payable. The role suited him well. He was brilliant at math, and he enjoyed working alone.

One morning, when he was 26, he met a girl at the bus stop. They were both taking the bus to work. They had a pleasant conversation that day, and from that time on, they sat together and became well acquainted. Stephen asked her on a date, and it went well. They dated for a while, then things became more serious. Eventually, Stephen got up the courage to ask her to marry him. He didn't really love her; he just thought it was the thing he was supposed to do in life.

She said yes, and they married. She had no family in California, which suited Stephen just fine in accord with his desire to remain out of the spotlight. He brought her to see his mother and brothers a few times, but the visits tapered off as the marriage was not progressing well. Stephen's twisted sexuality and his low level of desire caused problems for his wife. After two years she divorced him.

Stephen retreated into his solitary life, until four years later when he married again. He did not love his new wife either, but he understood that he needed to have a family. His dad would expect that of him. But the marriage did not go any better than the first. There were no children and even less intimacy. Stephen suspected his wife was cheating on him. He could never prove it, but after several years they formally ended the sham marriage.

During the following year, after his second divorce, Stephen, now 35, spent a lot of time alone drinking. He would frequently pull out the article he received so many years earlier about his dad breaking out of prison. He felt trapped inside himself, with no idea how he would get out.

Finding out that his dad was alive put an ever-present dark cloud over his life. He felt pressure to live up to what his dad would expect of him. He began to fear that someday his dad would come around and find out just what he was, what Mary said he was, a pussy boy! He had no wife, and no girlfriend to prove otherwise.

It was later that summer when he got another suspicious letter. This time too, there was no return address, but it was postmarked from Oklahoma. He carefully tore it open and glanced at the signature. It was from his dad.

Stephen,

It's your old man! I miss you boy. I've always had high hopes for you. I was going to take you with Mary and me before those FBI shitheads caught me and ruined everything. I hope Mary treated you right after I left. She told me she did, but I know she can be a real piece of work sometimes.

I know I haven't always been there to protect you like I wanted to. I'm sorry about that. I would have except those government bastards locked me up.

I can't see you now, the risk is too high cause I'm still running from the law. I hope someday I will find a way.

But I remember that country concert, where you tried to help me fight those country assholes! I was so proud of you boy. It's one of my fondest memories of you. I know you got it in you to be even greater than me.

Don't ever let anyone screw with you. You stand strong. Remember who our enemies are Stephen. Remember all I taught you.

Love you son,

Dad

Stephen finished reading and closed his eyes. He felt an enormous sense of pride. His dad really did love him and more importantly, still believed in him. But more than anything, he felt a sense of relief because his dad would not be coming around. The pressure of his dad coming to find out about his miserable failure of a life was off. That night, as he lay awake in bed, Stephen began to think about all the things Mary Jaycox had said to him. Someone was lying.

Oklahoma

Mary and Benny were living in Oklahoma currently. She knew about the letter Benny sent to Stephen, but Benny would not let her read it. She knew Benny wanted more than anything to be reunited with Stephen. Mary always knew it was what drove him, but it didn't worry her anymore like it used to. They were never going to see Stephen, she'd make sure of it, and that suited her just fine.

What worried her were the events of that night so long ago. Benny had unmistakably stamped some of his meanness into Stephen, but it was worse in the boy, and Mary knew he was downright evil. In one sense, she believed he was still that scared little boy pissing his pants with a gun to his chin. But in a broader sense, she remembered he had been there to murder her, just like he murdered those cats behind the cottage. It was a night she would never forget; just as she would always remember the evil in his eyes when he brandished that knife at her.

37 *Bingo Bruce*

CHAPTER 32

Theresa Mae: 1986, In the Beginning...

On an early summer morning, in a suburb of Cleveland, Ohio, Mark Connor saw Marie Russo for the very first time. He had heard from his parents that an Italian family lived next door, and when laid eyes on Marie, he could not stop staring at her. She had beautiful dark hair, dark eyes, and a lovely figure. The next morning, he and Marie were both walking to their cars that were parked on the street.

"Hi," said Mark. "My parents just bought the house next door here."

"Hi, I'm Marie." She looked shy as she spoke.

Mark tried to strike up a conversation by asking her for directions, but she could not help, so they casually said goodbye just as fast as they had said hello.

A week later he went to visit his parents again with hopes of seeing Marie, but she was not around. A few days later, Mark backed out of his parents' driveway and turned to head up the street, then stopped. In the neighbor's drive stood Marie looking cute as could be, wearing a large shop apron and oversized work gloves. She was standing next to her dad who was seated on an upside-down bucket. There were some tools and a small tarp covering the drive. He had the car jacked up with a tire off and was working on the car's brakes.

Mark watched for a moment as Marie handed her dad a tool. He rolled down his window, said hello, and waved. Marie smiled and started to wave, but her father instantly looked over his shoulder and muttered something under his breath in Italian. Marie quickly looked right back down at the brake job, momentarily glancing up, then back down again.

Mark found it all strange and drove off, but from that moment he could do nothing to get Marie off his mind. Mark knew he was in love and he just had to get to know her.

A week later while visiting his parents, he was outside their house getting something from his car when he noticed Marie pull in her drive. He saw his chance to finally talk to her alone. She was on her way to the house when he walked over and caught her attention.

Mark smiled, "It's funny isn't it."

"What?"

"Our parents live right next door to each other."

Marie had no reply, she just smiled.

Mark then asked, "Hey, do you like to play tennis?"

"Not really."

Mark scrambled, "Well, do you ever work out?"

"Yes, sometimes."

"Really, where?"

Marie sighed, "Scandinavian Health Spa."

"No kidding, I just got a pass there." Marie did not reply, so Mark pressed on, "Would you like to go there with me tomorrow?"

She sighed, "I'll think about it." She turned and began walking away.

When she was near the door, Mark called out, "Hey… how am I supposed to know what you're thinking?"

She stopped mid-stride, turned, and with a forced smile said, "Pick me up at 1."

The following day Mark came to the door and knocked. A short, stocky Italian man walked slowly to the door. He had the face and stature of Danny DeVito, only meaner and stronger looking.

In a thick Italian accent, the man loudly asked, "Whadda you want?"

"I'm here for Marie."

The little man glared at him through the screen. Mark glared back, or down, you could say. With Mark being 6'5", the man in front of him, intimidating in his own right, was only 5'3". The uneasy standoff ensued for a very long complicated entirely silent minute. Finally, the man jerked his head up toward the stairs and shouted, "Marrreeeee!"

Marie came running down the steps with a little bag in her hand. It was as if she had been hiding at the top, waiting for someone to say 'go.'

She wore a shirt she had gotten from a bank. On the front, it said, 'Electronically yours.' On the back, it read, 'Check it out.' Mark got the message, and a whirlwind romance ensued. For the next several weeks they spent as much time as they could together, going to the movies, going for walks, going out to eat. They realized they could not live without each other. So, after only 27 days, Mark proposed, Marie accepted, and they married six months later.

They wasted no time starting their family, and within 3 1/2 years later had four children, the second of whom had light brown curly hair with a cute Angelic face. They named her Theresa Mae.

38 *Mark and Marie Meeting Place*

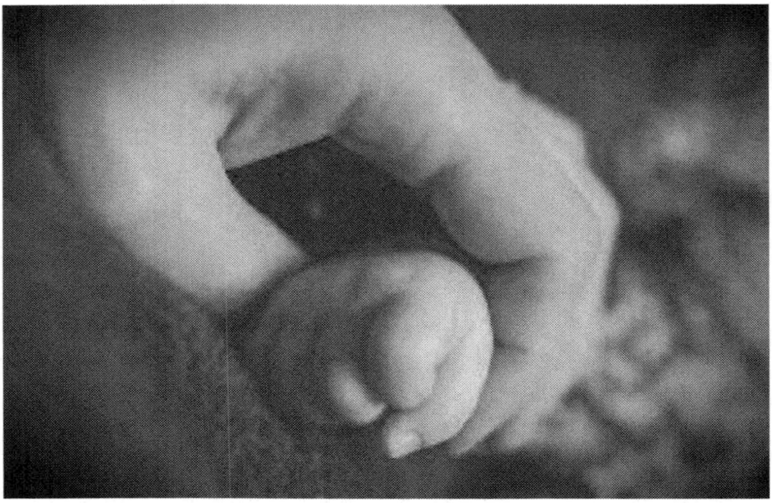

39 *Theresa Mae is Born*

40 *Stephen Paddock*

CHAPTER 33

During his late 30s and early 40s, Stephen developed a penchant for gambling. His genius-level math aptitude and understanding of statistics allowed him to easily beat the dealers and machines at most Vegas casinos. He also became adept at online gambling, especially online poker. Within several years he parlayed $100,000 in savings into almost half a million dollars. Gambling was fast becoming his life.

Because he could afford it, he began taking more and more trips to Las Vegas. He was a high-roller and often received numerous perks and notoriety amongst the staff. Complimentary rooms, show tickets, and meals from the casinos were often given. Although he was highly thought of, little was known of his real thoughts. His true endeavors were always kept secret.

One night in Las Vegas when he was 46, he was staying at the Atlantis hotel. Stephen placed a call to the escort service he utilized at times. Within two hours a tall, beautiful woman stood at the door. He let her in and took care of paying her.

She told him her name was Brandy. She had long silky black hair and a beautiful sensuous face. The only problem was her hair was throwing him off, but he brushed it aside. He got undressed and sat on the edge of his bed, asking her to strip in front of him. She undressed slowly as he had asked, then smiled, and began moving toward him. But at that moment, Stephen had a flash of memory. He realized her black hair reminded him of Mary Jaycox. He stopped her and looked down to see he was not aroused. He suddenly felt the gun Mary stuck into his chin and saw the puddle on the floor from so long ago. He pushed the woman aside, "You can leave."

"I can wait a little while. It's OK, you're just nervous."

Stephen glared at her, "Get out."

The sudden harshness of his tone alarmed her. She quickly dressed and left.

A half hour later the phone rang. It was the escort service. "Mr. Paddock, this is John from Exquisite, was there something about the last escort you didn't like?"

"I want a blonde or a red-head next time. No more brunettes."

"Very well Mr. Paddock, would you like someone there tonight?"

"No."

The next evening Stephen called again, and this time a voluptuous blonde-haired woman showed up at his hotel door. Stephen could see by her devious smile that she would do almost anything. He invited her in. Stephen undressed and sat on the bed, nervously noticing he was not responding. He told her to strip extra slowly. She did, and this time, he did not see Mary, but he could not get it up either. "I'm sorry. I'm not able… I'm not feeling well."

The woman seemed disappointed. She knelt in front of him. "You let me worry about that."

Stephen only remembered the prostitute kneeling in his back seat so long ago. He tried to push it out of his mind and concentrate. The prostitute kept working at it, trying to get him erect, but nothing happened. Stephen finally said in a frustrated voice, "Just get out of here."

She got up and left. Stephen called the service and told them to take him off their list.

The embarrassment he felt over his failure to perform drove him into a rage. His fire was burning out, and he had yet to prove himself to his dad.

In the spring of the following year, when he was 45 years old, Stephen received another newspaper clipping in the mail. It was about his dad. It was a tiny article that said Benjamin Paddock had died. Stephen wept reading it. He called in sick to work and spent the next several days quietly grieving. He knew now he would never be able to prove to his dad who he could be. He would never have the chance to prove himself.

But another part of him felt strangely relieved because deep down he was afraid that Mary might be right, that he might never measure to his dad.

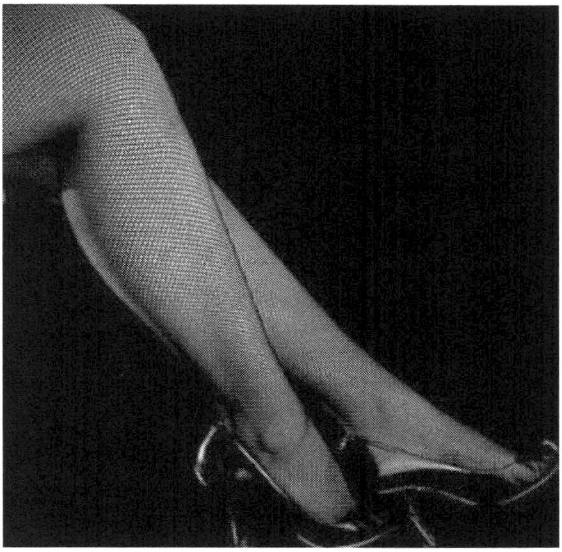

41 Escort Service

CHAPTER 34

Theresa Mae: Early Family Years

Around the time Theresa was 6 years old, the family bought a home on W. 135th Street in a lower middle-class neighborhood right next door to St. Vincent DePaul Church and School. Every day they would hear the church bells ring each hour from morning until evening. It was a constant reminder that God was watching over them.

Mark and Marie were devout Catholics, and living next to the church in the inner city with four small children made life special. In those days, when evening came, Marie and Mark would gather their children just before dusk, and light a candle in front of a statue of the Blessed Mother they kept on the mantle. They would go around and allow each child to say the name of someone they wanted to pray for. The children were always excited when it was their turn to lead the Our Father and the Hail Mary.

But it was story time that was the children's favorite. Classic short adventure stories were drawn upon nightly. As soon as the children got their evening snacks, Mark would begin to read, stopping to act out a pivotal scene out like "where the hunter was standing, and how he was holding his rifle when he heard the low growl of the man-eating tiger right behind him." His antics mesmerized them all. Stories were never started and finished on the same evening. Instead, Mark would find an exciting place to stop, then look up with suspense saying, "And we'll find out what happens tomorrow night."

The collective cry of the children was expected every night, and yet new and wonderful each time it was heard.

42 *St. Vincent DePaul Cleveland*

43 *Marie, Mark, and family. Theresa Mae with arm around her brother.*

CHAPTER 35

Theresa Mae: The Fire!

As Theresa and her siblings grew, the family continued to live their sheltered life under the umbrella of the nearby church. But on June 1, 2000, everything changed. Mark got the kids up that morning and helped Marie get them off to school. He went to work, and a few hours later, called home to see how she was doing. At one point in the brief conversation, Marie said, "Mark hold on a second, I have a call on the other line." She put him on hold.

Mark waited at his desk, occasionally looking at his cell phone, wondering what was taking so long. Suddenly his secretary called in, "Mark you have an emergency call from your wife."

Confused, he picked up, "Hello?"

"Mark, oh my God, the house is on fire."

He jumped up, "What, are you ok?"

Marie began sobbing, "I'm ok, I'm in the street out front, someone gave me their phone. Mark, the house is burning down!"

"I'm coming!"

He bolted out through the office and out the door. He drove the 33-mile trip doing over 85 mph. When he reached home, there were police cars and fire engines everywhere, along with a large crowd of people. Mark parked as close as he could and ran up to the house staring in shock. The fire was extinguished. All that remained was a smoldering blackened shell with water dripping from a hundred places on the heap of debris that was their home. A friend ran up, "Mark the kids are all at school. Everyone is safe."

"Where's Marie?" He yelled.

Someone pointed, "She's over there."

Mark ran to her, and they hugged for a long time. Both were in shock, yet they knew deep down that everyone was safe, and that was all that mattered.

That summer the family made a lot of decisions, including looking for a new home. One day they informed both sets of parents they had bought a house. They picked them up and loaded them into the van with their children and drove off. After driving for ten minutes, they headed back and pulled in a drive five houses down from where their parents lived, on the street they had met on. Everyone was overjoyed, after the trauma of the fire, the whole family was together now.

From that time on, life took a whole new direction for them. Suddenly the family was in the middle of the bustling suburbs, loaded with programs, libraries, schools, and sports available for youth. Along with all of this came public schools, and an immediate widening of all of the children's horizons in terms of friends and interests.

44 The Fire

CHAPTER 36

In the summer of 2002, Stephen decided to gamble on real estate. He purchased the run-down Central Park Apartment Complex in Mesquite Texas at a very low price. He set to work restoring the units and insisting only people with proper credit could rent there. Things turned around quickly and eventually an uptick in the economy, along with the improvements in buildings and operational changes, meant a windfall for Stephen. He turned the complex into a profitable machine, generating over a half a million a year. Around the complex, he was friendly, outgoing, and helpful, but he never revealed his real darker self to anyone. Stephen knew how to keep secrets.

The influx of money from the apartments helped to fuel his growing gambling addiction. Stephen was different than most gambling addicts. He worked hard to hone his math and statistic skills to serve his ability to continuously weigh the odds. Being a loner, with no real outside interests helped him to be more successful than most. Late night, and sometimes 'all-night' gambling proved effortless for him.

His success in these endeavors began to fill the void left by his lonely life. He still heard the voice in his head, but somehow, he was able to keep it at bay.

2007

Five years later, in early 2007, Stephen hired a new leasing agent to work at the apartment complex. Her name was Karen Mills, and for Stephen, it was love at first sight. Because of her, he began visiting the complex more often. He was mesmerized by her deep-blue eyes and light-brown hair. But it was her smile he loved the most; it captivated him every time he saw her. Every time he talked with her, he found a joy and a hope about life he had never knew before. He began to believe that perhaps there could be real love in his life.

Within two months on the job she received a raise, and three months later she received a second one. She was also given more and more responsibility, not in a more work sense, but in a more authoritative sense. It was fast becoming a career-defining job for her, moving her into management.

Karen could tell her boss had an overly keen interest in her, but she did not feel attracted to him. Besides that, she already had a serious boyfriend. Over the next year, she received numerous perks from Stephen, including raises and a generous expense account. On her one-year anniversary, Stephen surprised her with the use of a leased company car.

For Karen, work was going great, and she was happy to work with such a generous boss. For Stephen, Karen was the secret love of his life. The fact she was 11 years younger than him did not matter. The light and happiness he found when he saw her was driving him to improve himself. He was becoming less reclusive, and the episodes of rage were becoming few and far between. His gambling addiction also seemed to have less and less of a hold on him. He still visited Vegas often, but the all-night online part that used to fill his empty life was becoming less and less.

2009

During this year, Karen's boyfriend began to get jealous of all the attention Stephen was paying to her. He demanded she stop accepting all the gifts. She agreed, promising to talk to Stephen. When she told Stephen, outwardly he told her he understood, but inside he was devastated. Yet within a few days, he realized he had found something within himself. He realized he was capable of falling in love. He honored her request, but he never could let go of how he felt about her; he just kept it as his own secret.

2010 - 2012

Having fallen in love with Karen made it easier for Stephen to fall in love again. He was at one of the casinos in Vegas when he met a woman from Austin Texas named Linda Cranstal. She was six years younger than Stephen and good-looking for her age. She had short blonde hair and blue eyes… almost like Karen's.

Linda told him from the start she was not interested in any romantic relationship, as she was happily married. But she came to Vegas to gamble often by herself and loved to have friends. They spent a lot of time together the next couple of days, gambling, dining and taking in shows. She found Stephen to be funny, rich, and most importantly, she could tell he wasn't trying to get her into bed.

They met again four weeks later and had another fun weekend before returning to their own lives. After their third trip, they began texting each other, keeping each other's spirits up. Stephen was genuinely happy for the first time in a very long time. Karen slipped from his mind, and Linda Cranstal took her place as his crush. He was falling in love with her, and that love brought a lifetime of despair to a halt.

Despite his impotence, he tried going back to the escort services. But he only had random success, more and more he was failing to perform. Somehow though, the rage did not come to him. His love for Linda kept it away.

Things continued with them periodically meeting in Vegas for over a year and a half. On one trip in the summer of 2013, Linda was unusually quiet at the restaurant they were at. Stephen asked, "Are you all right?"

"No, not really."

"Well, what's wrong?"

"It's my husband. He says he's met someone. He says he doesn't love me anymore. He wants a divorce."

Stephen replied, "I'm sorry to hear that."

Linda took a deep breath. "I'm not. He has not loved me for years, I've just been pretending things would get better. It's over."

"Well, what are you going to do?"

"I'm going to divorce him, and get on with my life." She took a sip of her wine.

Stephen felt fear; he did not want to lose her. He loved her, but he was worried about more than losing her. "Get on with your life?"

She reached her hand across the table, grasping his. "Stephen, you've been a dear friend to me for over a year now. I'm grateful, and I want to keep meeting just like this. I need it, I need friends to get me through this time."

Stephen sighed, he felt profoundly relieved. "You can count on it. Now let's get out of here and go grab a show!"

CHAPTER 37

Theresa Mae meets Brie

On a warm September afternoon just after Labor Day, Theresa was on her way home from her first day of school, when she heard a voice calling from behind her, "Hey, wait up."

Theresa turned to see a skinny girl with long blonde hair and big blue eyes running toward her. "I wanted to say hi, I'm Brie."

"Hey, Brie. I'm Theresa."

"Hi Theresa, by the way, I love your hair. It's so curly. Is it a perm?"

Theresa smiled, fluffing her light brown curly hair, and laughed, "No, all natural."

"Nice," said Brie. "We just moved onto your street a week ago."

Theresa exclaimed, "Oh, are you that new family over by the Gravens?"

"Yes, they're our neighbors."

"Cool," said Theresa. "Are you in 8th grade?"

"Yes," said Brie, "are you?"

"Yes, but we must have a different schedule. I didn't see you in any of my classes."

"No, I'm not in any of yours, I looked for you. Hey, can you stop by my house and meet my mom? She just bought a pack of ice cream sandwiches."

"OK," said Theresa. They walked for several blocks passing up a few of the football players who were sitting at a bus stop. Brie waved at them, Theresa got out a half-wave.

After they passed, Brie said, "Ohhh… Eric Schantz is so cute. I just met him today, and I'm already in love." She looked at Theresa wide-eyed as a smile crept across her face. She was waiting for Theresa to smile and as soon as she did, Brie started laughing. Theresa shook her head, "You're funny Brie."

"I try," said Brie, smiling, flipping back her blonde hair.

They walked a little further and arrived at Brie's home only 11 houses away from Theresa's. Brie burst in the front door, throwing her backpack down, and shouting, "Mom, I'm home."

"I'll be right up," came a voice from downstairs. In a moment, Brie's mom came around the corner and up the stairs. "Welcome home honey. Who do you have with you?"

"This is Theresa, she lives right up the street."

Brie's mom gave a warm motherly smile and extended her hand, "Well it's nice to meet you, Theresa. Come on in. Sit down."

Brie started to make her way to the kitchen chairs, "Mom, can we have an ice cream sandwich?"

"Of course, you can," Brie's mom said, walking to the refrigerator, and returning with the ice cream and some other snacks. They talked and ate, laughing at some more funny things Brie said, until Brie pushed her chair away from the table, saying, "Hey, come on upstairs, I want to you show you my room."

"Don't be long Brie," her mom chimed in from the living room, "I have to take you school shopping in a little while."

"Sure mom, c'mon Theresa."

Brie raced up the stairs with Theresa following right behind. She ran to her bedroom door, put her hand on the knob, and waited for Theresa to catch up. "Ready?"

"Yes!" Theresa said, smiling.

"Take a look." Brie opened the door and stepped in, extending her arm slowly around the room.

Theresa looked around. On every inch of the wall were posters of what looked like country music singers. Almost all had cowboy hats and held guitars. "Who are all these people?"

"Country music singers!" she started to point all around. "That's Blake Shelton, these here are the Rascal Flatts, they're so awesome." Brie put her hand over her heart, "Look over here, that's Brad Paisley. I'm totally in love with him."

Theresa laughed, "I thought you said you were in love with Eric Schantz?"

"Well yeah, but not like I am with Brad Paisley." Theresa giggled out loud, shaking her head slowly back and forth. Brie too burst out into a wide smile. "Here, listen to this."

Brie walked over to her CD player and pressed play. A song began to play that Theresa had never heard. Brie sat on her bed, her eyes half closed, swaying back and forth. Theresa leaned against the dresser, listening. Halfway through the song Theresa asked, "Who is this?"

"It's Rascal Flatts, *I Melt*. It's one of my favorites. Do you like it?"

"Yes, I do, it's good," Theresa said, nodding.

"Well welcome to country music. I just know we're gonna be great friends."

They heard Brie's mom yelling up the stairs for them to come down. Brie yelled, "OK mom! I'll be right there!"

They made their way downstairs, and Brie said, "Thanks for coming over, I'll see you tomorrow."

"Sounds good, see you tomorrow."

As Theresa Mae walked home, she was thinking about the cool music she had heard, but more than anything, she was happy she'd made a new friend.

45 *Middle School*

46 ***Country Western Guitar***

CHAPTER 38

For the rest of 2012 and into early 2013 Stephen and Linda kept meeting in Vegas frequently. He was genuinely in love with her, though he would never say it. As the relationship continued, his anxiety over his impotence was growing. But his love for her was so strong, he did something he vowed he would never do. He went to a doctor to see what could be done for his problem.

As soon as he was in the room alone with the doctor, he made him promise that their discussion about his impotence would be left off the record. The doctor agreed, and after a lengthy discussion in which Stephen shared bits and pieces of his childhood, the doctor gave him his recommendation. He told Stephen that he believed that his fear of intimacy might be the reason for his impotence. He recommended Stephen seek psychological counseling to properly address his condition.

Stephen knew instantly he would not seek psychological help. Instead, he found a Canadian pharmacy online and ordered Viagra. When it arrived, he immediately went to Vegas, checked in to a hotel and called an escort service. He took the pill and was ready when the woman came. To his surprise, it worked. He went home the next day, excited at the possibilities that now lay before him. A week later he went to Vegas again. This time though, it did not work. He continued experimenting on his solitary trips, but more times than not it failed.

Stephen and Linda continued to meet frequently in Vegas. He was truly happy, as she never expected anything other than his friendship.

In the Spring of 2013, after taking in a show on the Vegas Strip,

Linda unexpectedly called down to his room late at night and invited him to her room for a drink. Stephen said, "Sure, I'm just getting out of the shower. I'll be up shortly."

Stephen's heart immediately began to race. He fumbled through his suitcase and took out the Viagra. He took a pill, then went into the shower. While in the shower he thought of all the times he had failed to perform with the escorts. He thought of that escort with the long black hair like Mary Jaycox. He started to sweat, even though cool water was running all down his body.

He quickly stepped out and dried off. The phone rang, Stephen raced over and picked it up. "Yes?"

"Hey, are you coming up?"

"Yeah… I'll be right there." More panic ensued. He could not calm his heart. He sat on the bed and thought of how happy Linda made him feel. He slowed his breathing and started to feel a glimmer of peace; he began to calm down. He got up and went to the elevator to go up to her room on the next floor.

He walked down the hall toward her room, trying to breathe slowly, trying to calm his nerves. He reached her door and knocked.

Linda opened the door. To his surprise, she was standing before him wearing only a black negligée. She stepped forward, put her arms around him, and kissed him. He began kissing her back, moving into the room, kicking the door closed with his foot.

For several minutes they kissed passionately where they stood. Stephen felt himself getting aroused; Linda could feel him too. She started moving them backward toward the bed, helping him unbutton his shirt as they went. They broke apart, taking a breath, as she laid back down on the bed, watching him shed his remaining clothes.

She sat up and pulled him down on top of her. They kissed some more, but Stephen suddenly realized he was not responding fully. He kissed her more, as she began to fondle him, but still, nothing happened. His mind was on fire screaming with the remembrance of all the times he had failed.

After several minutes, he sat up on the bed, "I'm so sorry. I love you. I've loved you from the first time I saw you. And I want you, but I just can't right now."

Linda took a deep breath, trying to calm her spirit. She felt very vulnerable at that moment. "Is this just a one-time thing, or do you have a problem?"

Stephen was honest. "I've had a problem, but I never cared, because I've never been in love before."

Linda was quiet for a moment. She smiled, nodding, and said, "I understand Stephen. You're a wonderful man, but at this point in my life I need to be loved physically, not just emotionally." She got off the bed and walked to the dresser, and was quiet for several moments. She turned around, with a half-smile on her face. "I don't think we should see each other anymore. But it was enjoyable while it lasted, and I'll always remember you, Stephen. I'm sorry, I really am."

Stephen nodded, he was too embarrassed to even think about blaming her for ending things. He knew that he could never be angry with her. He put his clothes on quickly left without saying another word. He went up to his room, packed, and checked out that night.

47 Linda Calling Stephen to Come Up to her Room

CHAPTER 39

Stephen got on the next flight out of Las Vegas to Dallas. It was early in the morning when his plane touched down. He retrieved his car and drove home.

Stephen got out of the car, went into the house, and fell onto the couch. He was physically, mentally and emotionally exhausted. Being rejected and humiliated in front of Linda had traumatized him.

It was late in the afternoon when he finally woke. The rage that had so long controlled him now burst forth like a collapsing dam. He screamed and pounded his fist into the wall, breaking a hole through it. "Damn her, goddamn all these women for letting me feel this way! And that damn Mary Jaycox, pointing that gun at me!" He knew full well all his troubles started when she humiliated him that night so long ago. Never mind that he had tried to kill her, that was irrelevant to him, it was still her fault.

He fell back, sliding down the hall with his feet landing against the door. He had just lost Linda, someone he truly loved. He crumpled up on the floor, weeping and lamenting all the terrible things that had caused him so much pain, it was too much to bear. Finally, he fell asleep.

From far away, the Dark Lord Legion felt Stephen's boiling rage resurface. That night he immediately came to visit Stephen, watching him, studying his mind as he slept. He saw that

Stephen was ripe for the picking and he began to forcefully shape his dream. In his dream, Stephen saw Mary in the cottage behind their old house. This time he had the gun, and he held it under her chin, laughing at her as she stood on her tiptoes, frightened. He pulled the trigger, but suddenly he was thrust into another dream, where he entered the cottage again. This time he grabbed her by the throat before she could scream and beat her mercilessly until she was almost dead. Stephen woke up abruptly, covered in sweat, and felt the rage still growing. Then he heard the voice in his head whisper. *Find her.*

He got up, wiped the sweat from his brow, turned on some lights and opened his laptop computer. He methodically opened a private browsing tab in Google and began typing, Jaycox, Mary + California. He scanned the results, flipped to the images tab, and made his way down the page. Nothing. Next, he typed Jaycox, Mary + Arizona. Nothing. He tried Oregon, Nevada, Illinois, Chicago, Texas, finally an hour and a half later, he tried Colorado. Before hitting search, he thought, *I will find you Mary Jaycox unless you're already dead and rotting in Hell!*

He clicked and waited for the listings to come up, then scrolled down. There was nothing. He went to the images tab and scrolled down. He stopped, halfway down on the page there was a picture of a group of older women in a stretching class. One woman looked to be about the right age and physique, but she was partially blocked with only half of her face and neck visible. Stephen zoomed in his browser. He knew what he was looking for and he found it. On the neck of the woman was a small tattoo, confirming it was Mary Jaycox. *I promised you I'd find you.* Stephen never promised Mary anything, only in his mind.

He drilled down on the photo looking for clues. On the back wall he spotted the name of the facility, and after researching further, he discovered it was near Colorado Springs. Stephen went more in-depth in his search now, and after only five more minutes found her address, 11723 Grey Goose Lane, just outside the city boundary. He checked the distance, she was only eight hours away.

Stephen had thought about this day countless of times. He began to perspire as he felt the rage building stronger than it ever had. He heard the whisper in his mind, *revenge.* He went upstairs, took a small bath towel, and cut it into several long strips. He rolled them all up neatly and put them in his pockets.

Next Stephen sat at his computer and opened a blank document. He found a legal form on the internet, copied it, pasted it into the blank document, fixed the wording, added some places for signatures, and printed two copies. Stephen smiled, he was pleased as he placed the forms into a manila folder.

There was only one more thing to do. He went into his room and grabbed his pistol from the drawer, and put it in the back of his pants like his dad used to. He then went outside, got into the car, and started driving.

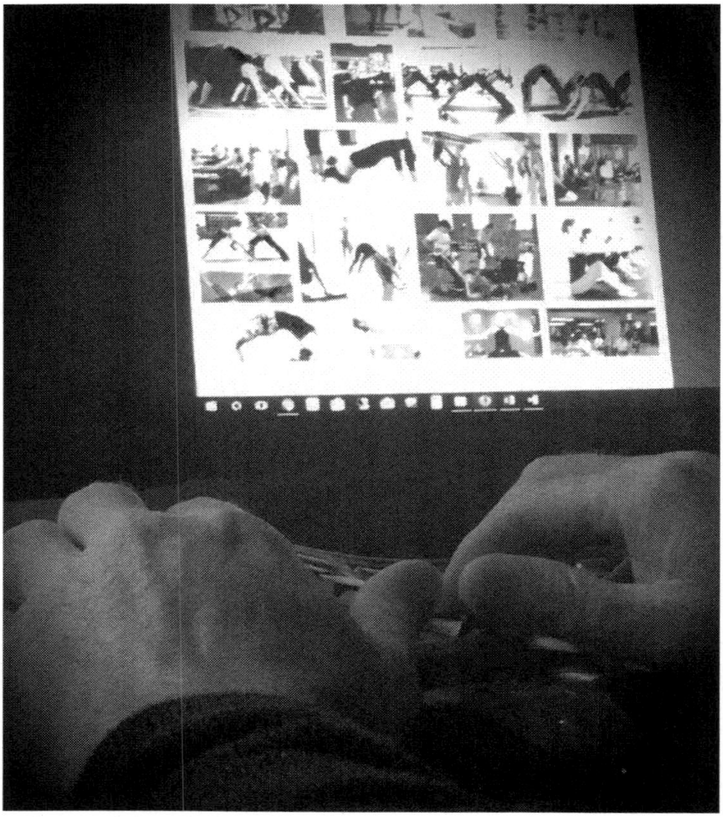

48 Stephen Searches for Mary Jaycox

CHAPTER 40

Stephen drove straight through the night, stopping only twice to grab a coffee and hit the restroom. He made good time and neared his destination. He turned onto Pawnee Avenue, then left on Red Mountain Lane until he reached Grey Goose Lane. He turned left again and quietly pulled in front of the light blue ranch. It was 5:53 a.m. It was still dark, and there was no movement in the neighborhood. He looked on the porch and saw the old metal porch chairs they used to have in Tucson and realized that she must have taken them the day she left.

Stephen pulled into the driveway lined with tall bushes on one side, and quietly got out. He tried to open the screen door, but it was locked. The pick-lock tool in his pocket wouldn't help. He went around to the back of the house, but the screen there was locked too. He went back to his car and waited. At 6:30 it began to get light. He saw the kitchen light turn on, then the living room. Stephen quietly got out of his car, went to the front door and knocked.

Mary Jaycox looked through the window in the front door. Her face became angry and surprised at the same time. She froze for a moment, pondering what she should do. It had been 15 years since Benny had died, and 43 years since she had laid eyes on Stephen, yet she instantly recognized him. She swallowed hard, then decided she'd see what he wanted.

Mary opened the door slightly, leaving the chain on, only enough to talk. "What do you want?" she asked.

Stephen could see the chain bolt still attached, and he knew he had to appear friendly, and be convincing if she was going to open the door. Stephen kept his voice low, and calm, so as not to alarm her, nor disturb any neighbors. "We need to talk Mary. My mom died a few months back. There are some legal matters to settle regarding my mom and dad's store. We just sold it."

"Well, what the hell does that have to do with me?" She eyed him suspiciously, watching for any sign.

"He left a provision in the ownership records stating that you're entitled to 10 percent of the net proceeds. The attorney sent me here to have you sign these papers and make sure we have your information correct so he can send you the check." He paused, "We are legally bound to try to find you in order to close everything and receive our stake."

Mary thought for a few moments. *Benny, he left me some of the store, God I miss him.* "How much money are we talking about?"

Stephen pretended to look at the papers inside his folder, then looked up and said, "$11,340." He half smiled.

Mary paused, looking him over for a moment. She unlatched the door and unlocked the screen. She walked quickly over to the living room ahead of him and sat down in her chair. "Sit there," she said, pointing to the couch just across from her. She already knew her gun was sitting right next to her, though he could not see it.

Stephen looked down at the papers. "So, I just have to confirm," he paused, "the check should be made out to Mary Jaycox?"

"Yes."

Stephen nodded, half smiling, but he was burning inside. He wrote down her name on the papers he brought. He looked up, barely able to keep up the façade any longer, and said, "You were with my dad till the end. What did he really think of me?

Did he say anything before he died?" Stephen sat carefully, so as not to dislodge the pistol in his pants. He added, "I want you to be honest."

Mary was going to forgo it, because of the money, but the temptation was too great. "To be perfectly honest, he blamed you for his going to jail. He pulled that last job against my wishes. He said he had to do it for you and your momma."

Stephen's rage was screaming in his head. He tried to keep a calm expression. "Mary, he told me he was going to take me away with him. He told me that right before he left that day. Was it true?"

Mary paused. She was so tempted to stop, but she couldn't, her old age had made her even crasser. "You really want to know what he said? I'll tell you but you're not going to like it." She sat up straighter, so she would be able to grab her gun faster, and said, "He said you were too far gone a momma's boy. He said there was no fixing you. He knew you'd never measure up to be a real man. What did he call you? Oh yes, I remember now, 'a pussy,' he said, you were 'a pansy pussy boy.' He didn't love you or your momma at all. He loved me."

The rage began to boil. Stephen clenched his teeth and said in a mean, low voice, "I don't believe you. Take it back."

Mary began reaching down the side of the chair, but not as fast as she had that fateful night so long ago. Stephen was faster this time. He jumped up, grabbed her arm, and twisted it. At the same moment, he yanked a strip of the cut-up towel from his pocket, and stuffed it into her mouth, immediately muffling her ability to scream. He then jabbed her hard in the stomach to get her to stop fighting back. Mary's eyes now began to water.

Stephen stood and yanked her up, binding her arms together with the other strips. He tied another strip around her head, holding the gag in, then pushed her back into the chair. He knelt and grabbed her struggling legs, binding them together. He then turned off the lamp and sat on the edge of the coffee table in front of her. The light from the kitchen allowed them to see each other clearly, but it made it hard for anyone outside to look in.

Stephen took a deep breath, the voice was now screaming in his mind. He clenched his fists and watched her horror-stricken eyes. "You bitch," he said as he cocked his gun and stuck it under her chin. "You did this to me, you did this all to me, and to my family. What do you have to say?"

Her eyes seemed to plead for mercy. Stephen's smile only widened. He loved seeing her in fear, getting what she deserved, what she gave him. He enjoyed it for a few moments. Then a concerned look came over his face. "Mary isn't it time for your morning bath. You seem so feeble, I'll help you today. We wouldn't want you to fall and hit your head in the tub. That would be just terrible."

He towered over her as he stood and picked her up, slinging her over his shoulder. He turned and strolled down the hall toward the bathroom, careful to keep her writhing body away from the walls. He wanted no marks on her body. He turned on the bathroom light, and walked in, making sure the window was closed tight. He then set her down very gently into the bathtub.

Mary stared up at him with a mixture of fear and hatred in her eyes. She tried desperately to break free of the bonds on her arms and legs, but knew it was no use. After a minute, she stopped, out of breath, with tears now running down the sides of her cheeks. She looked at him with only pleas for mercy on her face.

Stephen put the lid of the toilet seat down and sat on it, silently staring at her, his breathing becoming labored. He wanted to scream the rage was so great. But he knew his plan had to go flawlessly, so he calmly reached over and turned on the hot water, then the cold water, and put in the drain plug.

Mary's eyes widened as she focused on the water coming out of the faucet. She began to shake with panic taking over her face, struggling to get free again.

As the tub was filling Stephen reached over and gently rubbed her blackish-gray hair, smoothing her bangs off her forehead. It was time to make the bruise the coroner would want to see. He grabbed the top of her head and said, "This is for Irene." He slammed her head against the back of the ceramic tub, making the bruise the coroner would attribute to her falling. Mary writhed in pain with her eyes rolling behind her head for a moment, then closing.

Stephen smiled, folded his hands, and waited for the water to rise. He saw Mary come to, instantly her face held the cry for mercy. Stephen wanted to smash her head again, but he calmed his mind, remembering his plan. He closed his eyes, thinking of all the times he had killed her in his mind. After seven long minutes, the tub was sufficiently full, covering her entire chest up to her neck. His eyes flashed open, "OK Mary, it's time. This one is for my brothers." Stephen put his hand on her head and pushed her under, holding her there for almost 20 seconds, until she finally took water into her lungs. Then he pulled her up.

Now he addressed her, as if he were in a courtroom, or a board meeting, "Mary Jaycox. I hereby wish to give you one more chance to set the record straight. If you do, things may go well for you. But don't scream, or it certainly will not go well. Do you agree to this Mary Jaycox?"

With both horror and a glimmer of hope etched all over her face, she nodded.

Stephen untied the rag around her head and pulled the half-soaked towel out of her mouth, she coughed and gagged incessantly.

"Now Mary, do you wish to correct your statement?" Stephen

waited as she took another breath.

Mary coughed up water again, then nodded, collecting herself for what would be the most important words she ever spoke. She closed her eyes for a moment, as if deciding, then opened them and looked up at him. "Benny always thought one thing about you." She took another breath.

Stephen's heart began to race. He knew she'd been lying to him. "What is it? Tell me now!"

Mary nodded again, and glared directly at him, saying, "He said, you were a pussy!" She spat in his face and yelled, "Fuck y… "

She never got to finish as Stephen was ready. He forcibly pushed her head back under the water and held her down. She screamed, but the water poured into her lungs, and only bubbles came up, drowning out any sound. Stephen let up on the force, careful not to mark her, just to hold her, until she finally froze in her death pose. He kept his hand on her head, laboring to breathe, feeling a deep sense of relief, he had not felt since he killed the prostitute so many years earlier.

Stephen waited another minute, then carefully removed the bonds and took off her clothing. He pulled a black garbage bag from his pocket and put her clothes inside. He threw a bar of soap in the water and a washcloth, then dried the floor and wiped any prints from the bathroom. He went into the living room, and neatly put her gun and remote where they belonged, wiping any fingerprints away. He stepped over to the side of the front window and peeked through. It was quiet. He left out the back, locking the door behind him, got in his car, and drove away, feeling better than he had in years.

49 *The Bath Tub Where Mary Jaycox Met Her End*

CHAPTER 41

Theresa Mae Growing Up!

On a warm spring day in 2013, Theresa's father, Mark, sat on his back patio reading over a rough draft report he prepared for a client. It was then that he first heard it. He stood and walked over to his daughter Theresa's open window. He yelled up toward the window, "Theresa!"

No answer.

He yelled louder, "Theresa!"

Theresa's smiling face appeared in the window. "Yes dad?"

"What is that on the radio?" he asked.

"I don't know what you mean?" she replied with a little smirk on her face.

Mark asked, "Is that country music?"

Theresa laughed, she knew her dad was making fun of her. "Dad, I love country music!"

Mark smiled, "You like country music, are you joking?"

"Dad I told you… it's the best."

Mark launched into his fatherly duty to "lecture" his children. It was his way of keeping things light with them. "Theresa Mae, may I remind you, we are a Catholic family, and we listen to the Rolling Stones, AC/DC, Led Zeppelin, and groups like that.

Now, will you please go and change the station."

"Sorry dad, not gonna happen!" she said smiling as she slid the window closed.

Mark smiled, proud of her, knowing she was growing up.

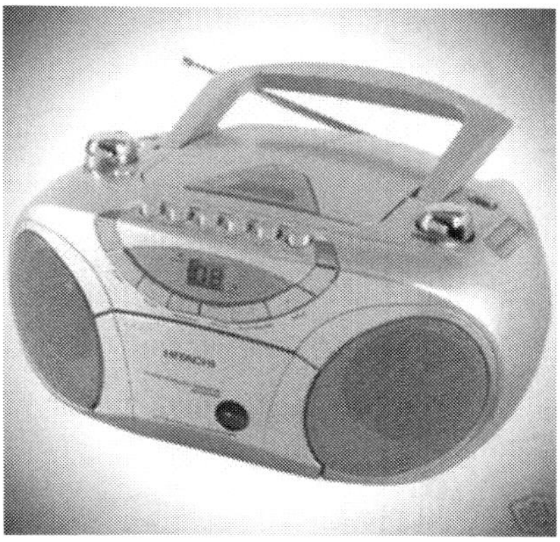

50 Theresa's CD Player

CHAPTER 42

After murdering Mary, Stephen began to spiral into a deepening depression, the worst he had ever faced. Long days were spent in bed tossing and turning, unable to sleep. His nights were spent playing video poker online, wagering throughout the night hundreds of thousands of dollars and winning several thousand almost every night.

He would take breaks from gambling, and scour pornography sites, trying to get off on sex of all kinds. Some nights he could, but most of the time he could not, which only enraged him. His impotence was getting worse. Many nights he would become furious, throwing things around, breaking countless items in his house. It was all he could do not to smash every breakable thing he owned.

After these tirades, he would open a bottle of scotch and start to drink. He was not an alcoholic in the traditional sense, but he had to drink just the same. He was afraid and unable to fall asleep because of a recurring nightmare that now visited him frequently.

In his dream, he walked through the concession area at a country concert stadium, like the one he, his dad and Mary Jaycox had gone to. He saw the men and boys who had beat them up standing around. Stephen would flip them off, and give them a special smile, which conveyed revenge. He would continue past them, and suddenly find himself in a long hallway, like the ones at the Vegas hotels. He entered a room, closed the door, walked to the bathroom and placed his hand on the bathroom door. He would hesitate because he knew what was waiting for him on the other side. He opened the door, turned on the light and saw Mary Jaycox sitting up in the tub of water, wearing her wet nightgown, staring at the faucet. She would turn her head and look at him with hatred on her water-logged face. Her words were always the same. "You're a pussy boy Stephen. You're coming with me… you're going to Hell with me!" She would then burst out into hideous laughter. The dream always finished that way.

It was at this time in his life that Stephen recalled his dad's gun collection. For some reason, it never seemed important to him, probably because he never got to use the guns with his father, as his dad had promised they would someday.

So, he went down to a local gun shop and purchased two guns. One was an older snub-nosed pistol, just as his father carried in the back of his pants. The other was a rifle. Stephen brought them home and admired them for days. Frequently brandishing them around his apartment, pretending to shoot people, especially the people he hated. Doing this connected him to his dad somehow, even though he understood he would never rob a bank, or try to gun down a lawman like his dad had. From that time on, he began buying all kinds of weapons and eventually rented a storage unit north of Dallas, where he built a display rack like his dad had, only bigger.

He began visiting the storage area at least twice a week, and it was always a thrill. He would step inside, close the door, turn on the light, and marvel at the rows of handguns, rifles and semi-automatic weapons he had accumulated. He knew his dad would be proud of him because he had more guns that were much more powerful than his dad ever had.

Later that year, in 2013, he sold his apartment complex in Mesquite, Texas. He made a sizable profit on the sale, making him now richer than he had ever been. He tried to make it in Dallas, but the depression would not subside. He decided to move to Florida to be closer to his family, but he kept his storage facility north of Dallas.

Stephen knew that being close to his brother's family and to his mother was a good distraction for him. He was always good at pretending; it was his way of coping as a loner. But since he was around family more, he had to work harder at it.

After moving to Florida, Stephen started getting more serious about online gambling, some nights putting as much as a hundred thousand dollars through all the myriad of bets he made. He always won something, it was his primary source of income now.

Along with his growing online gambling success, he started making more frequent trips to Vegas, cashing in on all the complimentary services he earned. The trips were now a regular part of his routine, often going a few times a month, for days at a time.

When he wasn't in Vegas, he would spend time with his family. He fooled them into thinking he was happy and would spend lots of money on them at fancy restaurants. He would brag that he was, without question, one of the biggest online poker players in the world. He would further brag that he sometimes would bet several hundred thousand dollars in one night. He bet a lot, but his delusions made everything more significant than they really were. The lines were blurring for Stephen.

The deeper he got into gambling, the less he felt vulnerable to the rage. But the nightmares of Mary kept coming; Stephen had just learned to live with them.

CHAPTER 43

When Stephen was in Vegas, he kept to himself, acting slovenly and anti-social. He usually walked around the hotels with his beer-gut hanging out, wearing Nike sweatpants, and cheap black flip-flops. He didn't care about how he looked, only about how he played. Winning, not appearances, meant everything. It was the only distracting force in his life that kept him out of deeper depression. Appearing sloppy and anti-social was his way of keeping people away.

By the fall of 2015, life had become drudgery for Stephen. He kept his routines, slept when he could, and endured his nightmares. He was empty in so many ways, but there was nothing he could do. One afternoon, while walking through a hotel lobby, he met a Filipino lady. She worked at the hotel and recognized him. She walked up next to him, and greeted him, "Hello Mr. Paddock, how are you?"

Stephen recognized her. She had always greeted him at the entrance to one of the casinos where she worked. "Oh hi," he said. "I'm OK."

"I see you often, are you from here?"

"No." Stephen was unsure if he should say more, but he continued, "I live in Florida, but I come here a couple times a month. What is your name?"

"My name is Rosamie. I see you a lot." Rosamie smiled and giggled, "You're a very tall man, Mr. Paddock."

Stephen laughed, her giggle sounded cute to him. At that point, he impulsively asked, "Would you like to have dinner with me tonight?"

Rosamie bobbed back and forth, pondering, "Hmmm, yes that

would be nice Mr. Paddock."

"All right, I need to go up to my room. Where can I meet you?"

Rosamie said, "I can meet you right here at 5:30 when I get off my shift."

"5:30 sounds good, I will see you then."

They went to dinner, and Stephen listened to Rosamie talk all about her family. He had not enjoyed a conversation with a woman since Linda. Hearing Rosamie's stories about her Filipino family actually amused him.

The next week, she joined him again for dinner, and from then on, they began to have dinner at various hotels around Vegas at least twice a week. Rosamie began taking him out to dance clubs where her Filipino friends hung out. He was well-liked amongst her friends, even though he was quiet and rarely participated in their conversation. But they appreciated that when he was there, he always picked up the tab.

As the months went on, Rosamie grew closer and Stephen began to realize he needed her as much as she needed him. Being needed by a woman helped him to feel that Mary Jaycox was wrong about him.

He was also tired of going back and forth to Florida, so in early 2016, Stephen began to scout out the area around Las Vegas for a home. He noticed a town with the same name as his old apartment in Mesquite, Texas, so he took a trip there and shortly after that purchased a home in Mesquite Nevada, paying cash. A month later he rented a truck and drove up to his storage facility in North Dallas, loaded up all his guns, and transferred them to a storage facility closer to his new home in Nevada.

Stephen decided Rosamie would fit in well with his hopes to keep himself out of depression. One evening after dinner and drinks, he asked her to move in with him. He promised to provide for her needs; she only had to be his companion. Rosamie agreed. She moved in, and Stephen gave her a generous weekly allowance to spend on whatever she wanted.

Life felt right for him during those first few months of life in Mesquite with Rosamie. He still had the nightmares, but he could now live with them. But after a few months, on a stormy night when Rosamie was away visiting her daughter, Stephen began to hear the voices again.

He had just finished playing in an online poker tournament and was finished for the night. He had settled into drinking scotch and looking at porn sites. A woman on one porn site reminded him of Mary, and though Mary was dead, his rage began to build. It was the same rage he felt that night he killed her. He sat fuming in his chair, swishing around his scotch in the glass, when he heard the voice clearly say, *Mary is dead, good Stephen!*

Stephen smiled and clicked on a different site. He chuckled and answered the voice out loud, "I know, I killed her sorry ass." The voice whispered, *There are more… there are more to kill.*

Stephen took a long sip of his scotch, feeling his adrenaline pumping, basking in the sweet presence of the dark voice. He went to bed, happy he had made a connection again.

51 ***Legion***

CHAPTER 44

In December 2016, Stephen and Rosamie enjoyed a Christmas dinner together at a casino restaurant in Vegas. When they got home, Stephen suddenly felt a terrible pain in his left upper abdomen, causing him to double over on the living room floor. Rosamie ran to him, "Stephen, what is wrong?"

"Ahhh, my stomach hurts." He again moaned loudly, the sudden pain almost taking his breath away.

"Let me help you up," she said.

"No… no, get me the antacids from the cabinet."

Rosamie ran to the kitchen and retrieved the bottle along with a glass of water. Stephen took a few and laid on his side, holding his stomach. A half-hour later the medicine kicked in. Stephen got up, sat on the couch and turned on an NBA game. Later that night the pain came back, though this time he did not tell Rosamie, but instead took another handful of antacids, and also a handful of Ibuprofen.

This went on for a couple of weeks until finally, he looked up a local doctor and went to see him. The doctor examined him and said they would have to run blood tests. Stephen could see the look of concern on the doctor's face. Before putting his shirt back on, he told the physician that he wanted to talk with him in person as soon as the blood test came back. Two days later the office called, and Stephen brought what he needed, and went in to see him.

The doctor met him in his office. Stephen sat down, holding a small bag, and said nothing. The doctor sighed, "Mr. Paddock, your blood work shows a high concentration of cancer cells."

Stephen's eyes widened, as he felt his heart lurch. "What kind of cancer?"

"I can't tell from the blood tests, but based on the exam we did, and where your pain is coming from, there's a good chance it is pancreatic cancer."

Stephen nodded; he already knew how serious pancreatic cancer was. He took a deep breath. "Tell me about that."

"It's premature to diagnosis it, you have to go in for more tests to know for sure, and to see what stage it might be at."

Stephen shook his head, "Listen, doctor, I'm not interested in any more tests. I just want you to tell me, your best guess."

The doctor took a deep breath, "Like I said, based on your pain, I'd probably guess that it's pancreatic cancer."

Stephen nodded, "I don't want anything written down, I don't even want this visit or my last one on my record." Stephen opened the bag and reached in pulling out a bank-bundled pack of bills. "Doctor, there is $1,000 in this bundle. There's nine more of them in this bag. All I want you to do is tell me what to expect, and erase my record from ever being here. You'll never hear from me again." Stephen held out the money.

The doctor hesitated, "Mr. Paddock, I don't know if…"

Stephen did not let him finish. "Doc, this is simple, take this cash, tell me what to expect, and get rid of my records. It's not hard, I accept what's happening to me."

The doctor looked at him once more, then nodded, showing he agreed. He said, "If it's true that you have pancreatic cancer, you can expect a lot of pain. It looks to me that you may have six months, to a year, but it could go faster depending on what stage it's at."

Stephen stood up, and looked at him sternly and asked, "Can I count on you to keep these past visits out of my record?"

The doctor nodded, and Stephen handed him the bag and quietly left.

Stephen arrived home in a panic, he was suddenly out of time. Rosamie was at work, and he knew she would not be back for several hours. He began cursing, walking through the house throwing things, breaking things. His life would end before long and Mary Jaycox would be right about him. He had to prove himself to his dad, he had to do something, something that would redeem his sad life. His rage began to boil, so he grabbed his half-full scotch bottle, chugged what remained, and smashed it into the living room wall. Then he drove to his storage facility, turned on the light, sat in his chair, and wept until he finally fell asleep.

The Dark Lord Legion had been keeping tabs on Stephen. Legion felt the desperate turmoil within Stephen, and he immediately set his eyes firmly on him. This time he had something special in mind. He began to visit him frequently in his dreams. He turned up the nightmares about Mary and magnified their intensity. He also stirred up Stephen's hatred for the country boys who beat up him and his dad. Then Legion began to whisper the dark sweet voice into Stephen's head frequently. *Guns, ammunition, kill, kill, kill thousands, prove yourself.*

Stephen went online to a Canadian pharmacy and ordered a six-month supply of pain pills. He also began visiting his storage facility often. He would drink, take pain pills, admire his guns, and sometimes fall asleep there. But now his interest in learning how to shoot them went into high gear. He began attending local gun shows and frequenting local shooting ranges. He started to buy ammunition, and go a few times a week to practice shooting. He would bring different weapons and practice for hours.

It was at these ranges that he first learned that a semi-automatic rifle could be modified into a fully automatic rifle with only a few parts that could be purchased on the internet. Stephen did as the voice instructed and had someone at the range help him figure it out. Firing what in effect was a fully automatic machine gun thrilled Stephen like nothing ever had before, and it made him feel like a man, like a real man.

During the next few weeks and months, he felt the pain in his abdomen getting worse, and as it did, he felt his rage growing. The voice would come often. *You're running out of time. Prove yourself to your dad. Don't let Mary win.*

Thaddus noticed Stephen's health getting worse, and watched from a distance as the Dark Lord Legion's influence over Stephen grew. But Thaddus wasn't worried, yes Stephen was dying, but Stephen did not have the guts to do anything outrageous. But Thaddus was not going to take any chances. So, when Legion was not around Thaddus worked his client for his own ends.

Thaddus reasoned it all out in his mind. Because Stephen had the mark, Thaddus knew he was expected to get him into Hell, just like he had got Benny into Hell. But Thaddus worried about one thing. Because Mary had provoked Stephen at such a young age, Thaddus worried that Stephen's murder of the prostitute and his murder of Mary, might not quite enough to get him there. So, he decided to make sure by getting one more random killing in, a killing that would ensure Stephen would be condemned.

CHAPTER 45

Theresa Mae: Mid August 2017

Theresa pulled into the driveway and ran over to her mom who was working in the front flower garden. "Mom, I just got off the phone with Brie, she's getting engaged to Eric, and she asked me to be her maid of honor."

Marie took off her garden gloves and hugged her, "Congratulations honey." They walked into the house. Mark was sitting on the couch reading the evening newspaper.

Marie smiled, "Mark, Theresa has some news."

He put down the paper, "What's the news?"

Theresa proceeded to tell him. Mark said, "Well that's great. When's the wedding?"

"In the spring. But I have even more news. David called me today, he wants Brie and me to visit., so we are flying out to see him in Vegas at the end of September."

"That's nice," said Mark. He knew Theresa and David were the closest of his children and was always glad when they visited each other. Mark asked, "Does he have enough room for both of you?"

"Yeah, I just talked to him. And there's even more news, we're getting tickets to go see a country concert there."

"Who's playing?" Marie asked.

"My total favorites, Eric Church and Jason Aldean."

Mark smiled, shaking his head, "I should have known, a country concert."

"Well of course dad, what other kind of concert is there?"

They all laughed, knowing Theresa got a good one over on her dad.

52 *Promotion for Route 91 Harvest Festival*

CHAPTER 46

Legion sat in his villa on the southern shores of Hell on a balmy late September evening. His plans for using Stephen were all but set, except for one thing, Thaddus. Legion knew he needed to distract Thaddus for several days, or he might end up getting in the way. Then the idea came to him. *Sansa, yes, the ever-irresistible Sansa.* He closed his eyes and summoned his consort.

The Dark Angel Sansa arrived at his villa within minutes. She was Legion's favorite sex partner or slave you could say, for the last 100 years. Legion has possessed her will long ago.

She bowed, "Yes, my Lord, you summoned me?"

"I have an important mission for you. There is a low-level Dark Angel named Thaddus. I need you to seduce him, and distract him for a while."

Sansa immediately protested, "My Lord, can't another female Angel do this?"

Legion railed, "You dare to countermand my orders! I warn you, if you fail me, you will not be pleased with what happens."

He continued, "I will tell Thaddus that I am planning to involve his client Stephen in something substantial later this year and that I need you to get to know all about him. You will spend a few days with Thaddus, then seduce him, and lure him away from his client by the 27th, taking him far away until the feast of the Guardian Angels begins on October 2nd."

Sansa bowed and nodded.

The next day she and Legion flew to Stephen's house to meet Thaddus, who was in the backyard sitting on the fence waiting for them. When they landed, he quickly stood, "Legion, greetings to you."

"Thaddus, this is Sansa."

"I know of Sansa, she is well renowned." Thaddus bowed, eyeing her as he did. He had left out the part she was renowned for.

Inwardly Sansa grimaced, she now remembered who he was, and she was not attracted to him. It was over 1500 years ago when Thaddus was part of a team she was leading to cause trouble with an Emperor in the declining Roman Empire. Sansa could not remember all of the details, other than Thaddus annoyed her during the entire mission. This was going to be a chore for her. She smiled, "Thaddus, I do remember you. I look forward to working with you again."

Legion spoke, "I want her to get to know Stephen, as we will be using him later this year."

Thaddus kept smiling, and replied, "That will be fine." Thaddus already knew Stephen would be dead soon, so he was not worried.

Legion turned to Sansa. "Find me immediately upon your return, as I have another mission for you."

"Yes, my Lord," she said.

Thaddus was surprised to hear her call him this. Only the possessed followers or captives of Legion called him 'Lord.' Sansa was obviously one.

As soon as Legion left, Thaddus said, "Look, I don't care who you work for. This guy Stephen is a loser, and he's going to die soon. So, don't get your hopes up, I think you're wasting your time."

"Well that sounds good to me, I was hoping to hear that. I'll tell you what Thaddus, let's spend a day or two so I can get to know Stephen some. I can't go back early though, so we'll have to just hang out somewhere."

"How long do you have to stay?"

"Probably until the Feast of the Guardian Angels starts."

Thaddus nodded but was very suspicious of her mentioning a specific date. They went into the house, it was 11:30 a.m. in the morning and Stephen was still asleep on the sofa, he was dreaming, moaning in his sleep.

"What's wrong with him?" asked Sansa.

Thaddus shook his head, "He's tormented with nightmares. His father was somewhat of an infamous criminal. Stephen on the other hand, is a loser, and he's impotent, and he has cancer." Thaddus laughed. "He's all but worthless."

Sansa knew there was more to the story. Otherwise, Legion would not be involved. Suddenly Stephen shouted into the air, "Goddamn you Mary Jaycox."

Thaddus glanced over at Sansa, signaling to wait. Stephen stood up slowly. He looked tired, still dressed in the boxer shorts and tee shirt he had worn to bed. He walked toward his bedroom, and yelled, "You bitch!" He held his hands against his head as if he was being tormented, screaming, "I'm not! I'm not what you say!"

Sansa took a deep breath. She knew now why Legion had chosen him. He was full of rage, a rage that Legion would use for some grim ending. She looked over at Thaddus, "I see what you're talking about. What are his nightmares about?"

"They are about his father's lover named Mary. She humiliated him long ago, and he killed her a few years ago. Now she torments him in his dreams."

"He killed her? What happened to her?"

"He drowned her, and yes, she's in Hell. The poor woman, all she ever wanted was to be with Stephen's father, Benny. But, she's on the other side of Hell, and will never see Benny again. It's pure hell for her." Thaddus threatened to smile, waiting to see if Sansa got the joke. She didn't.

"Hmmm," said Sansa, she remembered five years earlier visiting another one of Legion's special cases, the teenager who shot up the elementary school; he was tormented too. Sansa was putting the puzzle together. She said, "Well it looks like you're right, he's worthless. Let's go look around Vegas, and we'll come back later."

"Sure thing," said Thaddus.

Sansa smiled, letting Thaddus know how pleased she was. She wasn't, though, she was scared of Legion and what would happen if she failed.

53 *The Dark Angel Sansa*

CHAPTER 47

Theresa Mae: Arrives in Las Vegas

Theresa and Brie touched down in Las Vegas on Friday, September 29th, and Theresa's brother David was there at the airport waiting for them. They had a beautiful first day, taking in an afternoon show, eating at a great restaurant, and heading over to the Route 91 Harvest Festival on Friday night to see Eric Church. It would be their first night, as they had tickets also for Sunday.

His concert was one of the most amazing experiences of Theresa and Brie's life. David was more than a chaperone though; he too enjoyed the excellent music and exciting energy.

The next day they slept in, and after a late breakfast, they went to see the Hoover Dam. The entire day all Theresa and Brie could talk about was how awesome Eric Church's performance had been. After sightseeing, they hung out by his apartment's pool the rest of the afternoon.

That night, they all went out to enjoy the nightlife on the Las Vegas strip, taking in a great restaurant, and going to see Cirque Du Soleil's performance before calling it a day.

On Sunday morning they went to the late morning mass at the Cathedral of the Guardian Angels and had brunch after next door at the Wynn Hotel. After brunch, they hit the pool for a few hours, then got dressed and went over to spend the rest of the day at the music festival. There were six other artists scheduled to play, including Jake Owen, Big & Rich, and a few others. But it was the final act of the night that Brie and Theresa were anticipating the most, one of their favorites, Jason Aldean.

Brie took several calls from her fiancé Eric as the crowd grew gradually larger, and the excitement was beginning to build. At one point, when it was nearly dark, the whole crowd was singing along to God Bless America. Theresa was in awe of how special it felt to be with so many wonderful people who loved America and who loved country music.

54 *Route 91 Harvest Festival Early Evening*

55 *Night Descends*

CHAPTER 48

Sansa laid awake in the bed of the luxury hotel in Rome, Italy counting the minutes. It was already the Feast of the Guardian Angels, October 2nd. She glanced at the clock on the wall and decided to wait a little longer, but at 3 a.m. she had had enough. She got up out of bed and announced, "I'm leaving."

"Where are you going?"

Sansa laughed, "Thaddus, I wasn't here for you, Legion instructed me to keep you here until the Feast of the Guardian Angels began, and it started three hours ago. I'm outta here." With that, she flew out the window.

Thaddus sat up, at first dismissive of her rant, but then he pondered her meaning. *Why would Legion want her to keep me until the feast?* He bolted up with wide eyes, *Stephen!*

He leaped out of bed, threw on his tunic and began to pace. He shuddered and looked at the time. She was right. It was 3 a.m. on October 2nd, the Feast of the Guardian Angels had begun. He sighed, knowing whatever it was, he was probably too late.

Then his eyes widened, "Wait, it's not October 2nd in Las Vegas, it's still October 1st, and its only 9 p.m. Thaddus left in a hurry, realizing Sansa had forgotten about the time difference.

As he neared Vegas, he headed for Stephen's location and was surprised to find he was at the Mandalay Bay Hotel. He went directly to the end room on the 32nd floor and walked in. His eyes widened, and he said aloud, "Oh my God." Scattered practically everywhere in the room were heavy-duty arms, surrounded by an enormous amount of ammunition. In one corner stood an automatic weapon mounted on a tripod pointed at the window. He thought, *How did these get here? Where is Stephen?* Thaddus ran to the tripod and looked down. *The Festival!* He looked over to his left and saw a door to an adjoining room, wide open. *Does he have another room?*

As he approached the door, he saw Stephen standing before another tripod, holding another automatic weapon, facing out a window pointed in the same direction. Stephen was eyeing the scope looking through the window down at the crowd below. He was looking at a small piece of paper and making adjustments to the tripod settings.

Thaddus walked into the room and was suddenly grabbed by the neck. "Thaddus, what are you doing here?" He recognized the ugly voice, it was Legion.

"Legion?" said Thaddus, surprised, as he turned his head to see him. "I'm here to help."

Legion put him down, fuming, knowing Sansa had screwed up, "I have this under control Thaddus."

"Yes, I see," Thaddus said, looking around, acting impressed. "What's the plan?" Thaddus tried his best to appear genuine in his desire to help, but inwardly he was panicking.

Legion responded proudly, "My hope is that Stephen will kill a thousand people tonight. It will be the largest mass shooting in history."

Thaddus smiled again, but he was suddenly in complete shock, "A thousand people? What can I do?" Thaddus wanted no part of this, he wanted to stop it, but he also needed to have Legion think he was on his side.

Legion didn't care. "Leave now Thaddus, you are not needed."

"Yes, Legion." Thaddus quickly bowed, and turned to leave, heading straight into the hallway. His mind was racing. *If you let this happen, you will be punished by the Lords, and your name will live in Dark Angel infamy with the Angels of Hitler, Stalin, and all the other mass killers of history. Do something.* Thaddus said aloud, "I've gotta stop him."

He passed through the walls and flew down the elevator shaft to the lobby. He found a security guard and whispered into his head. "Major problem on 32 at the end of the hall. There are guns! Go!" Thaddus stepped away and watched the guard go to the elevator and up to floor 32. The guard exited the elevator and walked swiftly toward the end of the hall, not knowing exactly why except he had a feeling something was wrong. Then he saw the cart outside the door, there was something on it, it was a camera. Thaddus whispered into his ear, "In there! He has guns, lots of guns!"

The security guard stepped to the side of the door and knocked, saying, "Security, open the door please."

Inside Stephen froze, turned, and looked at the door with a horrified look on his face. Legion barked into his mind, "Forget him, get started!"

Stephen ignored the voice in his head and picked up a rigged semi-automatic gun and started spraying the door with a hail of bullets.

Thaddus let out a great sigh of relief, at least now the hotel was on notice. He ran up to find the security guard wounded, laying in the hall. Thaddus raced back down to the lobby, shouting into the ear of any guard he could see. "Floor 32, there's a shooter on floor 32!"

He raced back up to the room, but Stephen had already started firing down onto the crowd below. Thaddus knew he would have to confront Legion, and he did something he had not done in thousands of years. He whispered a prayer to the Lords, a prayer for strength.

He then rushed into the room and saw Legion in his dark hooded robe standing just behind Stephen. Legion turned immediately with a look of evil anger on his face and ran at Thaddus. But Thaddus somehow possessed the strength he needed. He put out his arm, and caught Legion by the neck, stopping him, and thrusting him down onto the floor. He quickly picked up a machine gun, and as Legion tried to get up, Thaddus chucked it into Legion's head, knocking him out. As he watched Legion fall down, he saw Stephen walking behind him, heading toward the tripod in the other room, getting ready to begin shooting again.

Thaddus ran into the room after him, trying to figure out how he was going to stop him.

CHAPTER 49

Theresa, Brie, and David stood in the crowd 20 feet from the stage when they heard the sound of fireworks. Theresa looked around, suddenly feeling something moist on her face. Someone started screaming, and she saw Jason Aldean pause, and run off stage. She put her hand to her cheek and looked at her fingers. There was something red and warm on them, she couldn't understand, but she knew it was blood. She turned and saw David sliding down. She looked at his face and saw the agony, yet still did not understand what was happening. "David, what's wrong?"

She reached out to catch him, but at that moment, there were several more loud pops, causing her to look up. Just ahead of her there was an explosion of blood, and she saw a woman try to grab her bloodied neck, as she fell over. Many in the crowd began yelling. Theresa turned again to David, now seeing his bloody leg.

Brie saw him too, and she pushed past Theresa and grabbed David, helping him to lay down. Theresa looked down in horror, trying to piece together what was happening. She heard someone yell 'Oh my God, there's a shooter!"

People started screaming to get down, as the pops kept coming along with random bursts of blood. Theresa jumped down next to David and saw a hole blown in his leg. She screamed, "David!"

David opened his eyes and looked up at her, wincing. Everyone began screaming, running, shouting, crouching on top of each other, as the shots kept coming. Some started to run, while others heeded the voices to stay down.

The crowd was fast thinning out around them. Brie held David's head up, as Theresa yelled at the man next to her, "Give me your belt." He quickly took it off and helped Theresa tie a tourniquet around David's upper thigh. She asked, "David, can you walk?"

"No," he said weakly, closing his eyes again, trying to absorb the pain.

The shooting suddenly stopped. Theresa said aloud, "Oh my God, thank God." She looked at Brie. "We've got to get him to a hospital." She looked around, there were small groups of people everywhere, trying to help others. Blood was everywhere. "Brie, get out of here. Go get help, get someone to help us."

Brie squeezed her shoulder, locking eyes with her for a moment, and took off running toward the back of the concert field.

Within 30 seconds the shooting started again. Theresa scanned the field, and for some reason her eyes locked on a middle-aged man, running pulling his wife along behind him. She watched them for a moment when suddenly, the woman was struck in the chest, and she fell to the ground dead as her husband tried in vain to save her.

Theresa's eyes filled with horror, she turned to David. "We're going to get you out of here Dav… uhhh." She felt the thud as if someone had kicked her in the chest. Suddenly she could not breathe. She fell over on top of David. People nearby rushed to her side, turning her over. There was blood coming from her chest, she gasped, tasting blood as time suddenly seemed to slow. She heard their voices and knew it was bad. The bullet had struck her in the chest and ripped clean through. They were putting pressure on the wound, trying to stop the bleeding.

Everything went into slow motion, Theresa felt her heart racing, but she could not breathe, and everything was growing dimmer. She managed to look over at David, but his eyes were closed. Slowly her eyes closed too, as everything turned to black.

CHAPTER 50

Thaddus looked back into the other room, Legion was still on the floor knocked out. Thaddus was surprised and knew he only had a short time before he would wake. He ran to Stephen made himself completely visible to him and pleaded, "Stephen, you have to stop, the authorities are coming right now!"

Stephen was not seeing him or hearing him, it was as if he were in a trance. Thaddus wanted to kill him on the spot, but he knew he was not allowed to interfere directly. But he decided to intervene anyway, at least into the gray area, he would face the wrath later. He grabbed one of the weapons and jammed it, then he jammed another, then another, he kept going, making most of the guns in the room incapable of firing. He then picked up a machine gun and sprayed the door with gunfire again, so that Stephen would think that the police were on their way in.

He turned to Stephen, screaming, "Stephen, they are here, it's over. You can't let them take you alive. If they do, they will torture you, and find out what a loser and pussy you really are."

Stephen paused, and looked over at the door. Thaddus saw his efforts were working, and he continued, "They're coming in any minute, Stephen. Don't let them take you alive!"

Stephen picked up his snub-nose pistol, the kind he bought to remember his dad by, the one he brought with him for this exact purpose. He placed it near his mouth and paused. Thaddus exhaled, knowing the moment was near, "That's it, Stephen, that's it, don't let them take you alive. Just do it."

Stephen was hesitating though, and just then Legion woke. He immediately screamed out, "No Stephen, there are more to kill. No one is at the door! Get back and start shooting!"

Thaddus knew what to say, he leaned over into Stephen's ear, "If they catch you alive, they'll find all about what Mary Jaycox said about you, that you're a pussy boy!" Stephen heard him as his eyes widened in fear, he looked at Thaddus, and then over at the tripod pointed out the open window. He pushed the pistol deep into his mouth, grabbed the trigger, and pulled it.

Thaddus heard the thud of Stephen falling to the ground. He sighed, and glanced at Stephen's lifeless body, laying on the floor face up, with the back of his head blown off and surrounded by a puddle of thick blood and brain matter. Thaddus then stepped over to the window and looked out at the carnage below. He fell to his knees, with his face in his hands. He knew he would pay dearly for what had happened.

He then heard Legion shout, "I WILL put you in a dark cage for the rest of eternity for this Thaddus!"

Thaddus looked over, stood up, and walked right up to Legion. He grabbed him by the throat, still feeling his extraordinary strength, and said, "Fuck you Legion."

Thaddus let go, turned, and flew out the window, knowing it was now just a matter of time before they would arrest him.

CHAPTER 51

Theresa's eyes remained closed as time stood still, as all noise from the field faded. Everything was silent for several long minutes. She felt strange, and yet she felt more peaceful than ever before.

She opened her eyes reluctantly and found herself standing up in the same place, 20 feet from the stage. She turned around, slowly scanning the area. For the first time, she saw the carnage as bodies were everywhere. Everywhere were small groups helping others, there was blood all over, and everywhere people weeping over loved ones. She looked down and saw her own body laying still, her face covered up by a shirt. Next to her was David with his eyes closed.

She looked up again, and her eyes met those of an Angel, who was standing right in front of her. He had dark black hair and welcoming brown eyes and was smiling at her. He stretched out his hand, and she took it. They floated up slowly into the sky. Theresa was now able to see the entire field. She could not believe her eyes, and suddenly understood the magnitude of what had happened. She looked again at who was holding her hand and asked, "Who are you?"

"I am Anthony, your Guardian Angel."

Theresa felt sadness and happiness all at the same time. She asked calmly, "Where are you taking me?"

"To a special place not far from here."

Theresa held on tightly as she watched below and realized they were flying around the perimeter of the Las Vegas airport. Theresa watched in awe and felt the gusts of wind as several jets taking off flew right past them. She then saw a sizeable lit-up park not far from the airport, with four baseball fields and a beautiful small lake. Anthony smiled at her, "We are going down there."

"What is it?"

"It's a park… there's a couple of people who want to say hello to you."

They landed and walked by the lake. Anthony said, "Come with me, they will be here any minute."

As Theresa walked, she looked down at her clothing, everything was clean. Then she saw others walking or talking with Angels. Some were standing and looked like they were waiting, others were speaking to a small group, hugging, crying. Theresa could tell there were tears of happiness flowing, not just sorrow. "Who are those people Anthony?"

He lowered his head, and half smiled. "You will know soon. Let's go over here and sit."

They walked to a bench and sat down. Theresa sat down, but felt confused, she did not know why they were there. She looked at Anthony who was scanning the sky, suddenly he smiled and watched two people descend and land in a small nearby grove of trees. "They are here Theresa, two very special people who love you are here to see you."

Anthony took Theresa by the hand, and they walked into the grove. Theresa saw a short man and a woman standing together. She thought she knew them and yet they looked different to her. She walked closer, wondering, "Grandma? Nonno Cris?" It was her two grandparents who had died years earlier, but they were younger than she ever remembered seeing them.

Nonno Cris put his hand in the air, waving it, calling out his familiar name for her,"Tarrreeesa!!"

Theresa ran to them, and leaped into their arms, as they all embraced in a wondrous group hug. She kissed her grandmother, "Oh grandma I missed you so much."

Her grandma brushed Theresa's hair back, and held her tight, "I'm here Theresa, I'm sorry honey. Everything is going to be alright." Theresa nodded, and turned to her Nonno Cris and hugged him tightly, saying, "It was so scary, I don't know how it happened."

"Tareesa" he said in his thick Italian accent, "don't worry about anything. Everything's gonna be alright." He kissed her on the cheek.

Theresa turned to her Angel Anthony, "Is David going to be OK?"

Anthony nodded, "Yes, he's on the way to the hospital. I think he's going to make it."

Theresa suddenly looked around, as if she just remembered something. "What about Brie?"

Anthony said nothing but only looked down at the ground. He looked up after a moment and said, "I'm afraid she didn't make it."

"Oh... oh no." Theresa fell to her knees weeping, thinking of Brie and all her plans to get married to Eric. It was as if all the shock and wonder suddenly wore off. Her grandma knelt next to her, pulling her close, helping her to grieve. "Grandma, am I really dead?"

Her grandma hugged her tightly, "No Theresa, you are alive forever now." She held Theresa tightly, "You're coming to

Heaven, and it is the most beautiful place you will ever see."

Anthony waited a few more minutes and gently whispered, "It's time Theresa. We have another place to go."

Theresa looked up, teary-eyed, "Where are we going?"

"We have one more stop."

56 *Sunset Park, Las Vegas*

CHAPTER 52

Anthony helped Theresa to stand back up. She said goodbye to her grandparents, and she and Anthony flew together again over the skies of Las Vegas. After a little while, they saw a large church next door to the Wynn Hotel. In front of it was what looked like a giant red cross on the ground. They descended on it and walked to the front doors of the Guardian Angel Cathedral.

The three large doors were closed. Anthony opened the center one, and led her in, processing up the center aisle toward the front altar. Theresa suddenly remembered she had been there that morning before the concert. In the pews were other people, each sitting with an Angel. Theresa suddenly realized they were the other victims who had lost their lives.

She quickly turned around, scanning right, then left, then she saw her. It was Brie. Theresa ran towards her, shouting, "Brie! Brie!"

Brie looked up, wide-eyed, "Theresa!" Brie jumped up and ran to her. They both embraced, crying in each other's arms. Brie said, "Theresa, I tried to get help. I'm sorry."

Theresa nodded, "It's doesn't matter Brie, I don't understand it all yet… but I think we're going to be OK."

Brie nodded, then started crying again, "I already miss Eric, I am going to miss him so much."

Theresa pulled her close, "I know, I know. Brie, we're going to get through this together."

Anthony softly tapped Theresa on the shoulder, letting her know it was time for them to take their seats. They walked back to the center aisle and to a spot near the front and sat in one of the pews. Theresa looked back at Brie, then around at everyone in the church. She counted at least 50 people but knew she had missed several. Suddenly the entire wall of the church behind the altar began to glow, and in the place where the image of Christ was painted, it turned a fiery bright white.

Three beings, two male and one female appeared out of nowhere and slowly descended onto the altar. Following a moment after them was a woman in a white robe with a blue vale. She took her place, standing to the side of them. Next seven magnificent Angels, all dressed in dazzling white and gold uniforms with golden swords and golden headbands, some male, some female descended onto the altar and took their places surrounding the three beings. Theresa gasped in awe as she suddenly felt a warmth inside her.

Anthony leaned over, "Those are the Lords, and the Archangels of Heaven."

Theresa's eyes widened. She looked back at them and noticed one looked like Jesus. Then she realized the other male looked older, like God the Father. The female Lord she had never seen, but Theresa was in awe of her radiant beauty and the strength that emanated from her.

Theresa asked, "Is that one Jesus?"

Anthony smiled and nodded.

Theresa asked, "Who are the other two?"

Anthony pointed, "He is the Father, and she is the Holy Spirit."

Theresa was about to ask who the other woman with the blue vale was, but there was no more time.

The three Lords all raised their hands, as the female one said, "Receive the blessing of the Lords." Theresa suddenly felt an immense feeling of being completely accepted and completely loved wash over her. She could do nothing but close her eyes and bask in it. After a few minutes, she opened her eyes. The woman with the blue vale was looking at her from the side of the altar, smiling at her. Theresa leaned over to Anthony, "Who is that woman there?"

Anthony smiled, "You don't recognize her Theresa?"

Theresa looked at him, and began to shake her head, then stopped, "Is it the Blessed Mother?"

Anthony nodded.

Jesus spoke, "We are the Lords of Heaven. So much love was poured out from the hearts of people all over the world who stormed Heaven with their prayers, that we had to come and see for ourselves, and personally, welcome all of you into Heaven."

He paused, "You will now see the one who did this. He will face judgment, and so will the Dark Angels who allowed this to happen."

The back doors of the church opened. Everyone turned to see four Angels in uniforms marching in up the center aisle, followed by a disheveled looking man with a scraggly unshaven gray face. He was chained at his hands, and his legs were shackled. Behind him was an Angel with dark black shiny wings, he too was chained. He looked sad and very different than the other Angels. Four more uniformed Angels marched behind him. When they all reached the front, the others stood aside, leaving the chained man and the Angel standing before the altar.

Jesus said, "Thaddus step forward. You were condemned thousands of years ago, but now your punishment will be even more severe. What do you have to say?"

Thaddus trembled, he knew his fate could be decades in a dark cage at Holy Mountain, and then he would be sent back to Hell to face Legion's promised punishment. "Lord, I… I tried to stop him. I was deceived."

"But you were going to allow Stephen to kill one person, at least, isn't that enough?"

"My Lord, I have no defense, only that I tried to stop him from killing thousands. I… knocked Legion out, and I convinced Stephen to kill himself, stopping him, saving untold numbers of people." Thaddus glanced over his shoulder at some of the victims, and added, "I only wish I could have acted sooner."

The Lords looked at each other for a moment, then the one who looked like the Father nodded. Jesus too nodded, then motioned to two of his Angels. "Take him to a dark cage for the next 100 days, and then keep him in the place of reform for Angels until I can determine his fate."

Thaddus looked up in unbelief. He had been spared the punishment he feared, but he had received much more than that. While he knew a dark cage meant terrible suffering, even for only 100 days, he was not being sent back to Hell where he would face inevitable destruction. He had a feeling he was going to eventually receive mercy, and never have to return to Hell again. Two Angels then took him away.

Jesus then said, "Stephen Paddock step forward. You have committed a horrible offense against love, and humanity. What do you have to say?"

Paddock raised his eyes. He felt no remorse. He looked around at those in the church. He scratched his cheek with his chained hands, "I have no regrets about what I did."

Jesus took a deep cleansing breath. He closed his eyes for a moment as if in a moment of prayer, he never enjoyed condemning anyone, but he was the judge.

Suddenly a voice came from the pews, it was a woman. She stood up, alone and said, "I forgive him Lord." She then began to tear up, and she sat back down.

Theresa turned around to see her, and their eyes met. Theresa could not imagine how she could forgive him after what he did. Another person stood, and said, "I forgive him Lord." Then another stood, saying the same, then another, followed by more. Theresa sat there in shock listening to them. She knew full well what her faith said, to forgive those who wronged you. She tried to get herself to stand, to forgive, but she just couldn't, not after being killed, not after David being shot, not after seeing her best friend's life and wedding stolen from her. She listened as more people forgave Stephen. Over 30 victims, many in tears, stood, all saying the same four words, "I forgive him Lord." Then it grew deadly quiet, and all eyes turned to Jesus.

Jesus lowered his glance to the floor, he too had tears in his eyes. They were tears of happiness, as the love his followers displayed in the face of evil overwhelmed him. He looked at the other Lords and nodded. He waved his hand, and the back portion of the walls behind the altar opened again, this time wider. Beyond them, though it was night, all could see a bright shining land, teeming with all kinds of life and beauty floating in the distance. Theresa began to cry, she knew it was Heaven. Jesus looked to the seven Archangels, and said, "Splendora, Michael, step forward."

Immediately two of the Archangels stepped forward and knelt. Jesus said, "All of these people are granted eternal life and everlasting joy in the Heavenly world. Take them Splendora and

Michael under your special care and get them everything they need. They are to be taken at once to their new homes."

Splendora and Michael both bowed, turned, smiling and said to everyone in the church, "Follow us."

Suddenly, all the Archangels, Angels, Mary, and all of the people in the pews and their Guardian Angels lifted into the air and ascended up through the large opening. Then the roof and walls closed back up, and Stephen Paddock was left alone, standing in his chains in front of the three Lords.

Jesus moved one step closer. He looked at the back of the church. Legion was there in his dark hooded robe watching to see what would happen. Stephen stood perfectly still, with clenched teeth, staring blankly at Jesus' feet.

Jesus lowered his head to meet Stephen's eyes and said, "It seems many of my followers have forgiven you."

There was silence, Stephen showed no emotion, only the hint of a smile about to unfold. He said, "I don't care about them! I hate them all." He looked up defiantly, "I killed them didn't I!"

Jesus took a breath and exhaled very slowly. He appeared upset, and said in a heated tone, "Don't you know I have the power to condemn you to Hell, or to forgive you, and send you to a place where you can learn to love again, where you can learn to live life as you are supposed to live it."

Stephen paused for several moments, showing no emotion. He looked up and said, "Who are you to judge me?"

For a moment, Jesus face showed the disappointment he felt, but then a look of calm resolution came over him. He looked back at the other Lords, and then looked again at Stephen. Jesus then lowered his glance to the floor, thinking, saying nothing. He suddenly looked up, "Stephen, I am the judge of all men and all women who will ever live, and I do not forgive you. You are condemned to Hell."

With that, the Lords turned and disappeared out the same way they had arrived. Stephen stood alone in the church with a confused look on his face. From the back of the church, Legion raised his arm in the air, and two Dark Angels, each with a large hook flew up the aisle, and drove the large steel hooks into his shoulders, lifting Stephen off his feet. He screamed in agony with a pain he had never known.

Legion boldly walked up the center aisle of the church and up onto the altar in front of him. "Stephen, you fool, I wanted you to do more. Because you disappointed me, you are being taken to a special cell, where you will live with a very special cellmate." Legion smiled.

Stephen shook off his pain for a moment, and looked up, "My dad? Is it my dad?"

"No Stephen, it's not your dad . . . it's Mary Jaycox."

"Nooooo!" he screamed, as the Dark Angels lifted him into the air, allowing a dark hole to open beneath them. Then, they all dropped down into the dark as it closed above them.

57 *Guardian Angel Cathedral*

58 *Inside Guardian Angel Cathedral*

CHAPTER 53

Mark and Marie received word early the next morning that their daughter was dead, and their son was in the hospital but expected to survive. They immediately went over to Brie's house; her parents had also just gotten the news. They all grieved together for a long while.

That night, Mark and Marie took a flight from Cleveland to Las Vegas, neither of them able to compose themselves. Their first stop was to the hospital where they saw David. He tried to sit up and tried to put on a brave face, but as soon as they reached his bedside, they hugged, and all began to cry.

The following morning, they made their way to the coroner's office, where Mark and Marie, both identified Theresa Mae's body. Marie broke down, crying inconsolably, as her knees buckled, and she sank to the floor. Mark helped her up and took her back to their hotel room.

The next day Mark made arrangements to have Theresa's body flown home with them on the plane. They waited two more days until David was discharged from the hospital, as he too would be coming home with them. They all flew back together to Cleveland and mentally prepared for Theresa's wake and funeral.

The funeral was set for October 11th at their long-time family church, St Vincent DePaul in the old neighborhood where the family had some of its fondest memories together. When the day came, the church bells rang loudly, and the enormous group of mourners processed into the church and took their seats. Theresa and her Angel Anthony arrived from the sky and sat on the steps of the altar not far from her casket, facing everyone. Throughout the service, Theresa was crying, but not for herself, she was crying for them. They were the ones hurting, they were the ones who did not know what Heaven was like, and that she was OK now.

Theresa could not stop watching David, she knew him better than anyone else, he was called her Irish twin and was her younger brother. She was sad knowing what he was going through.

Anthony saw this, and he nudged her. "Go talk to David, whisper into his ear, tell him what you want to say."

Theresa wiped her cheek and walked over. He was seated in a wheelchair on the side of the front row. She put her hands on his shoulders, touching her forehead against his. She felt his pain, his guilt that he couldn't protect her, that she stayed behind to help him and lost her own life. She gently held the sides of his cheeks, looked in his eyes and said, "I love you, David, please understand, it wasn't you who needed me, it was I who needed to stay with you." She kissed his cheek and sat back down on the steps, hoping her words would lift his burden.

During the homily by Father Manning, a long-time family friend, Marie broke down sobbing. Mark pulled her close, holding her against his shoulder, as his own tears rolled down his cheeks. She needed her parents to know she was OK. She walked over and stood behind them, putting one arm around each of them, "Mom and Dad, I love you. I'm going to be OK. I promise."

Theresa drew closer and whispered in her mom's ear. "Mom I'm alive, and I will always be alive in your heart." Marie seemed to get ahold of herself, nodding subtly with eyes closed, as if she were hearing Theresa as if she was feeling her presence. Theresa closed her eyes and nodded and sat back down.

At the closing song, Theresa and Anthony stood and processed out behind the coffin. They followed the long line of cars below to the grave site and hovered in the sky. Here the crying was the loudest. Theresa turned to Anthony, "Why does it have to be so sad? Don't they know it's not me down there, it's only a shell of me that will turn to dust? Why don't they understand?"

Anthony put his arm around her. "They understand Theresa. It's just that they already miss you more than they can bear, and they know it will be a very long time until they see you again. He pulled Theresa closer with one arm and hugged her. "But one day, one amazing, glorious day, each of them will. They will hug you, and laugh with you, and sit down and hear all about you, and they will live with you forever. It's all coming, and it will be a glorious reunion."

Theresa took one more, long look at her mom and dad, and her brothers and sister, and her friends. She said, "Thank you, Anthony. I'm ready to go now."

She paused, taking in one last look, and with her eyes watering, she blew them a kiss. "I'll miss you all. Till we meet again."

59 *Saying Goodbye at St. Vincent DePaul*

CHAPTER 54

One Year Later

Theresa woke and walked out onto her patio that overlooked the Great Heavenly Sea. She took in a deep breath, taking in the sea air, then went inside and poured herself a cup of coffee. She came back out and stood by the rail looking out at the endless blue waves. It was quiet, and she loved it that way. It was the reason she woke so early this day. Today was the anniversary, it had been exactly a year since she had been ushered into her new life.

Theresa loved her life in Heaven and yet this morning, because of the anniversary, she felt sadness. No one was immune from remembering how they died, or their old life. It was part of their history, part of their story, part of being human. Adjusting to life in Heaven took time too, as it was all new. Only children seemed to effortlessly make the jump to Heaven without ever feeling sadness.

Theresa had a new family now, ancestors who loved her dearly, and wonderful new friends. She also was falling in love with a young man she met recently. But today the sadness was back, and Theresa yearned to see her mom, dad, and siblings again. She wanted to feel their warm embraces, to laugh at her dad's silly jokes, and work in the garden with her mom, to just spend time with David and her other siblings.

Deep down she was glad the sorrow was back. It had frequently surfaced during the past year, though its hold on her was lessening. It wasn't a painful sadness, but more a yearning for special days that were gone. But Theresa wanted to hold on, and she vowed she would. It was her way of holding onto them, her way of never letting go of those she loved.

She got dressed and made her way up the quiet tree-lined street in the southern portion of the First Heavenly Realm. It was still early on a beautiful spring-like Sunday morning, with flowers in bloom and birds chirping everywhere. Many people were already up and about, some on their way to visit friends, some on their way to worship services being held all over the Heavens. She was humming her favorite Jason Aldean song as she walked, waving and smiling at the people and Angels passing by.

She reached the house and walked up the sidewalk. She knocked on the door of the beautiful home overlooking a small river valley. She waited, turning to look at the beautiful landscaping in the neighborhood, then knocked again. Suddenly the door opened, and there was Brie.

"Hey, Theresa!"

"Hey, Brie! Gooooood morning!"

Brie was in her robe, and her wet hair was wrapped in a towel. She stepped outside and hugged Theresa tightly, "Come in, come in, I've missed you!"

"Brie! I just saw you a week ago."

"Oh my," said Brie. "Has it been that long?" They both started laughing. Brie turned, "Come on in, I made some breakfast for us."

Theresa walked into Brie's home when suddenly she stopped. On the living room wall was a poster of Eric Church. "Where did you get that?"

Brie smiled, "My Angel got it for me."

"Really! I want one!"

"Well, I'll let him know," Brie said, holding her hand out. "But I'll need 10 bucks."

"Ten bucks, for what?"

"Well you don't think he's going to steal it, do you?" Brie shook her head. "He has to buy it."

Theresa looked puzzled, "I thought everything is free up here."

"Yeah, everything is free up here. But they don't sell Eric Church posters up here!"

Theresa started laughing, and so did Brie. They hugged tightly, both still coming to grips with the immense newness of their life and the sorrow of remembering all those they missed. "Theresa said, I'll get you the 10 bucks, can he bring one up here?"

Brie nodded. "I'll make sure he gets you one. C'mon, let's eat breakfast, we have to go soon."

"I can't wait!" said Theresa. "I've been so looking forward to this."

"Me too," exclaimed Brie.

They ate breakfast and Brie ran up to quickly get ready. She came down dressed in blue jeans, a flannel shirt, and a pair of women's cowboy boots. She was holding a box behind her back.

Theresa stood in the living room watching her. "What ya got?"

"I got you something."

"What is it?" asked Theresa.

"Close your eyes," said Brie.

Theresa closed her eyes, and heard Brie fumbling with the box, and then felt something being placed on her head.

Brie said, "Keep them closed."

Theresa felt Brie grab her by the shoulders, "Keep them closed tight, and step over here." Theresa felt Brie moving her a few feet in the living room. "OK! Open!"

Theresa opened her eyes. She was staring into a mirror at a new cowboy hat. "Awwww! I love it. Brie this is awesome!" Theresa turned and hugged her, knocking the hat off as she did. "Oops." They both went to pick it up and bumped heads. "Brie!!" They started laughing and hugged again. Theresa saw another hat sitting on the chair behind them. "You got one too?"

"Well of course. Now let's go."

"Hey wait. Where's the list of who's performing tonight?"

"I have it right here." Brie walked over to her mantle and pulled off a card, along with two tickets. She handed it to Theresa.

Theresa looked it over and began reading aloud. "Don Williams, Troy Gentry, Oh I can't wait to see him. Let's see, Glen Campbell, Merle Haggard, Joey Feek." Theresa closed her eyes. "She is sooo pretty. I'm so excited to go." She looked at the card again. "Lynn Anderson, wonder who she is? George Jones and Tammy Wynette." She looked up, "Are they a duet?"

"I think so. I've haven't heard their songs, but I've heard this is going to be a *great* concert. I also heard they're going to start having them a lot more often."

"Really? That's awesome."

Brie added, "Well there's like hundreds of country singers up here. I never listened to the older ones, but I bet they're amazing."

"I know." Theresa looked down at the card, "Oh wait, the last performers are Johnny Cash and June Carter!"

"I know right!" said Brie. "What a beautiful love story, it still gives me goosebumps."

Theresa agreed, "We need to meet them tonight."

"Yes, we will, that's why we're going early. Are you ready."

They both put on their hats and went out the front door. "How far is it from here?" asked Theresa.

"It's about 30 miles, we're going to fly." Brie lifted, "Hold on to your hat!"

They flew north along the coast, admiring the beauty and vastness of the First Heavenly Realm. After about a half hour they saw it. On a giant lush green mountainside field below, looking out over the sea, there were thousands of people milling about. Everywhere there were small stands. It was early, so they knew they had lots of time to get something to eat, make some new friends, and depending on what time they arrived, possibly even meet some of the performers.

They landed and walked about the vast grounds, talking with folks, eating some delicious foods. In the early evening, the first performer came on stage. It was Lynn Anderson, wearing a pretty skirt a white top, blue vest, and cowboy hat. She stepped up and spoke into the microphone in front of over 200,000 people comfortably spread over a wide arcing field. "Good evening Y'all. Are you ready for some country?"

The crowd went wild. Lynn smiled her radiant smile and laughed. She turned to those behind the stage, smiling. Then her face grew more somber, "Before we begin, we want to remember the families of many of our dear loved ones still hurting after the tragic event in Las Vegas one year ago today. Please bow your heads."

Lynn began, "Lords of Heaven, we know you, and we know that you bring beauty out of ashes, you bring strength out of fear, you bring gladness from mourning, and you bring peace from despair. Help those on earth who are still struggling with the loss of that night, and who still need your tender loving care. We ask this in the name of the Lord who became one of us, and who I heard, loves country music, Jesus our Christ!"

Lynn smiled and looked out at the crowd, and asked, "Amen?"

The entire crowd lifted their heads and said in a resounding chorus, "Amen!"

Suddenly a man stepped forward with a banjo, and another two with guitars and they began picking and strumming furiously. Lynn brushed her hair back, and held the microphone close, and began to sing.

Wish that I was on old' Rocky Top
Down in the Tennessee hills
Ain't no smoggy smoke on Rocky Top
Ain't no telephone bills

Once I had a man on Rocky Top
Half bear, the other half cat
Wild as a mink, but sweet as soda pop
And I still dream about that

Lynn raised her hand high in the air.

Rocky Top, you'll always be
Home sweet home to me
Good old' Rocky Top
Rocky Top, Tennessee
Rocky Top, Tennessee

The men stepped forward again, strumming and playing louder and faster. The crowd was clapping along in rhythm. Theresa looked around, amazed at the scene. She turned to Brie. "Oh my gosh, I love this song!"

"Me too!" said Brie, smiling ear to ear, "Me too!"

Theresa heard the excitement in her friend's voice, she listened to the crowd singing along with wondrous joy, and she understood why. It was because the love, and the beauty, and the hope of Heaven, only glimpsed at in beautiful moments of their earthly lives, was now real and was now theirs forever.

A Note from the Author

I wish to sincerely thank you for reading my novel. Please give a brief **Review** of this book wherever you purchased it.

For more series info, join our Email List at

www.dpconway.com

or join our Advance Reader Team at

www.daylightspublishing.com

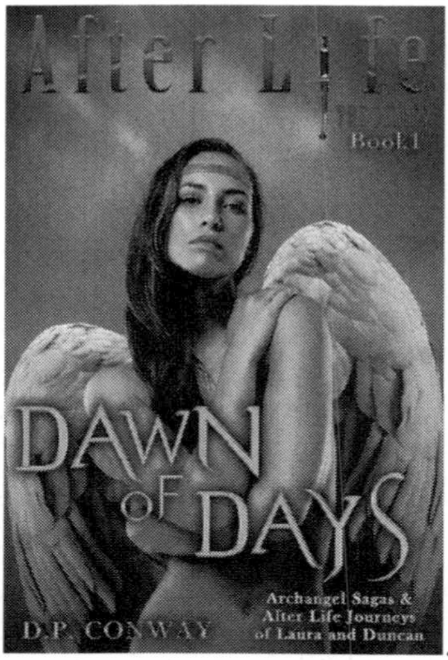

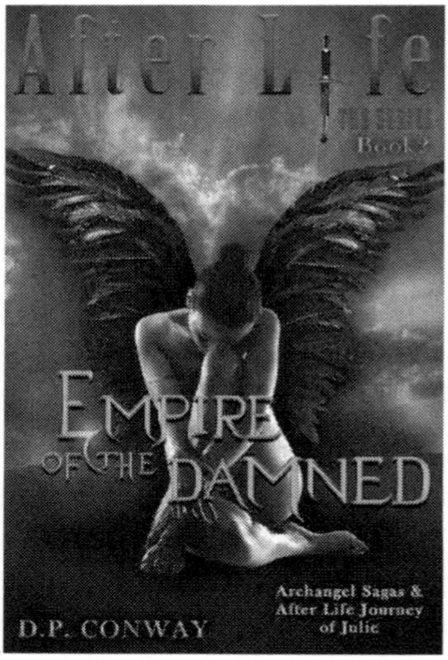

Book 1 Book 2

12 Novels in all in 2018 and 2019.

Who Trespass Against Us

Acknowledgments

For Marisa, your patience, encouragement, and love made all the difference.

Contributing Editor, Mary Egan.

Contributing Editor & Co-Publisher, Colleen Conway Cooper

Mary and Colleen, thank you for your excellent ideas and first-class editing. Having both of you carefully and tirelessly team up to shape and refine this book has made it as much yours as it is mine.

Concept Collaborator, Edward Markovich

Cover Design, Colleen Conway Cooper & Nate Myers

Final Editor Connie Swenson

After Life, the Series

Acknowledgments

For Marisa, my wife, your patience, love, and encouragement, made it possible for me to write this series. I love you more than these words can say… *Cara mia, Io ti amo. Solo tu femmina.*

For Carla Reid, who inspired the Archangel Splendora in the upcoming series with her strength and flare, but more than anything, with the joy of her constant friendship that can never be measured.

For Sadie Sutton, who inspired the lead character in the upcoming series, the Angel Sadie. You really must be an Angel, because meeting you changed me forever. Always…my friend.

For Ed Markovich, our associate, who has been a rock since the beginning, and who asked me to consider writing *Who Trespass Against Us*. Your excellent ideas Ed made this book great.

For Reda Nelson, our long-time associate, who helped keep the ball rolling, and moving through five long, difficult years.

For Mary Egan, our dear friend, who tirelessly insisted on rewrites and asked the questions that needed to be asked.

For Megan Franciscus who was a major force for shaping and editing half of the books in the series during the first three years.

Also, thanks to Jocelyn Caradang, Rosie Queen, Peggy Stewart, Mary Greene, Angela Rabbitts, Annette Joseph, Bridget Mae Conway, and all 50 or so test readers over the last five years.

Thank you!

Photographic Credits

1. William and Ellen Bury Home, Dundee (Courtesy of Wikimedia Foundation, Inc.)
2. News clipping of Ellen's murder, (DC Thomson, Ltd., 2018)
3. Sentence of Death for William Bury, (Courtesy of Wikimedia Foundation, Inc.)
4. Dundee Hanging Platform, (Courtesy of Dark Dundee History Archives)
5. Mrs. Marjory of Dundee, (Courtesy of Telegraph Media Group)
6. Benny Age 25, (Courtesy of Wikimedia Foundation, Inc.)
7. Ralphy Weinberg outside the Golden Rod Ice Cream Co., (Chicago Tribune, 2018)
8. Paul "the Waiter" Ricca, (Courtesy of Wikimedia Foundation, Inc.)
9. Roger Touhy and Gang, (Courtesy of Wikimedia Foundation, Inc.)
10. St. Boniface Cemetery (Courtesy of Archdiocese of Chicago)
11. Mary Jaycox, age 23 (Courtesy of Pinterest)
12. Era Maternity Hospital (irishcentral.com, 2018)
13. 4th of July Parade, (franklinrodeo.com, 2018)
14. Steinfeld's (Courtesy of Tucson.com)
15. Pima County Sheriff Badge, (Courtesy of Tucson.com)
16. Benny's Wall of Guns, (Courtesy of gunsmagazine.com)
17. Round Up Motel, (Courtesy of Round Up Motel)
18. Valley National Bank in Phoenix, (Courtesy of Valley National Bank)
19. Country Boys in Phoenix, (Courtesy of Wikimedia Foundation, Inc.)
20. Dark Cage, (Courtesy of apartmenttherapy.com)
21. Eva Dugan, (Courtesy of Wikimedia Foundation, Inc.)
22. Robles Girl, (Courtesy of Wikimedia Foundation, Inc.)
23. Dillinger Captured, (Courtesy of Wikimedia Foundation, Inc.)
24. National Bank in Phoenix, (Courtesy of Wikimedia Foundation, Inc.)
25. Irene Gets Her Money Back, (Courtesy of Wikimedia Foundation, Inc.)
26. Sheriff Burr, (Courtesy of Wikimedia Foundation, Inc.)
27. Benny Caught by G – Men, (Courtesy of Wikimedia Foundation, Inc.)
28. Benny In the News, (Courtesy of Wikimedia Foundation, Inc.)
29. Mary Jaycox Says Goodbye, (Courtesy of Wikimedia Foundation, Inc.)

30. Stephen School Picture, (LA Daily News, 2018)

31. Stephen Tennis Team, (LA Daily News, 2018)

32. Diner Near El Paso, (Courtesy of Wikimedia Foundation, Inc.)

33. La Tuna Federal Penitentiary, (Courtesy of Wikimedia Foundation, Inc.)

34. Most Wanted, (Courtesy of Wikimedia Foundation, Inc.)

35. Most Wanted, (Courtesy of Wikimedia Foundation, Inc.)

36. Prostitute, (Courtesy of adelaidenow.com)

37. Bingo Bruce, (Courtesy of Wikimedia Foundation, Inc.)

38. Mark and Marie Meeting Place, (D.P. Conway, 2018)

39. Theresa Mae is Born, (Courtesy of Konten dewasa)

40. Stephen Paddock, (Courtesy of Wikimedia Foundation, Inc.)

41. Escort Service, (Courtesy of Wikimedia Foundation, Inc.)

42. St. Vincent DePaul Cleveland (Courtesy of Diocese of Cleveland)

43. Marie, Mark, and family. Theresa Mae with arm around brother. (D.P. Conway)

44. The Fire, (John L. Bisol, 2018)

45. Middle School, (Unknown)

46. Country Western Guitar, (Unknown)

47. Linda Calling Stephen to Come Up to her Room, (Unknown)

48. Stephen Searches for Mary Jaycox, (D.P. Conway, 2018)

49. The Bath Tub Where Mary Jaycox Met Her End, (Unknown)

50. Theresa's CD Player, (Unknown)

51. Legion, (Courtesy of Wikimedia Foundation, Inc.)

52. Promotion for Route 91 Harvest Festival, (rt91harvest.com, 2018)

53. The Dark Angel Sansa, (Android apps on Google Play, 2018)

54. Route 91 Harvest Festival Early Evening, (Courtesy of Wikimedia Foundation, Inc.)

55. Night Descends, (Courtesy of Wikimedia Foundation, Inc.)

56. Sunset Park, Las Vegas

57. Guardian Angel Cathedral, (Courtesy of Diocese of Las Vegas)

58. Inside Guardian Angel Cathedral, (Courtesy of Diocese of Las Vegas)

59. Saying Goodbye at St. Vincent DePaul, (Courtesy of Diocese of Cleveland)

87859407R00141

Made in the USA
Lexington, KY
03 May 2018